burning
ambition
(a Hottie novel)

burning ambition
(a Hottie novel)

Jonathan Bernstein

razor
bill

An Imprint of Penguin Group (USA) Inc.

Burning Ambition

RAZORBILL

Published by the Penguin Group
Penguin Young Readers Group
345 Hudson Street, New York, New York 10014, U.S.A.
Penguin Group (USA) Inc., 375 Hudson Street, New York, New York 10014, U.S.A.
Penguin Group (Canada), 90 Eglinton Avenue East, Suite 700, Toronto, Ontario, Canada M4P 2Y3
(a division of Pearson Penguin Canada Inc.)
Penguin Books Ltd, 80 Strand, London WC2R 0RL, England
Penguin Ireland, 25 St Stephen's Green, Dublin 2, Ireland (a division of Penguin Books Ltd)
Penguin Group (Australia), 250 Camberwell Road, Camberwell, Victoria 3124, Australia
(a division of Pearson Australia Group Pty Ltd)
Penguin Books India Pvt Ltd, 11 Community Centre, Panchsheel Park, New Delhi – 110 017, India
Penguin Group (NZ), 67 Apollo Drive, Rosedale, North Shore 0632, New Zealand
(a division of Pearson New Zealand Ltd.)

Penguin Books (South Africa) (Pty) Ltd, 24 Sturdee Avenue, Rosebank, Johannesburg 2196, South Africa

Penguin Books Ltd, Registered Offices: 80 Strand, London WC2R 0RL, England

10 9 8 7 6 5 4 3 2 1

Library of Congress Cataloging-in-Publication Data is available

Bernstein, Jonathan

Burning ambition : a Hottie novel / Jonathan Bernstein.
p. cm.

Summary: Beverly Hills superhero Alison "Hottie" Cole, tired of dealing with conflicts between her sidekicks, accepts an internship at her favorite magazine, but fifteen-year-old Editor-in-Chief Pixie Furmanovsky seems determined to ruin her life.

ISBN: 978-1-59514-280-1
[1. Superheroes--Fiction. 2. Interpersonal relations—Fiction. 3. Internship programs—Fiction. 4. Journalism—Fiction. 5. High schools—Fiction. 6. Schools—Fiction. 7. Supernatural—Fiction. 8. Beverly Hills (Calif.)—Fiction.]
[Fic] 22
2009032552

Printed in the United States of America

To the Bernsteins of Glasgow

ONE

The Legendary Adventures of the Department of Hotness

The kingpin of the Belgian crime syndicate patted his luxurious thatch of midnight black hair into place and leaned into the video monitor, ready to be several hundred million dollars richer. He expected to see quaking, tearful representatives of his hostage's family carrying briefcases stuffed with bills, desperate to make the exchange and end their nightmare. Instead, he saw . . . a girl. A girl who didn't seem to be much older than fifteen. Wearing a red leather jacket, a short black cocktail dress, huge black sunglasses, and what looked like a thick gold chain that hung down to her waist and ended in a big burning *H*.

The girl looked straight up at the closed-circuit camera. She wagged a scolding finger at the lens. For a second, it seemed to the Belgian crime boss that flames had erupted from the girl's fingers and engulfed the camera. And then the image vanished, and the monitor was awash with static. The crime boss had no clue who the girl was or what had just happened. But he knew one thing. An intruder had breached his lair. The smooth running of the hostage handover was in jeopardy. He picked up his phone and said, "Get her."

Alison Cole stood in the middle of the abandoned warehouse deep in the San Fernando Valley and awaited her welcoming committee. In the months since she'd actively engaged in superhero duty, she'd come to relish the seconds of solitude before the fray. They allowed her time to focus, gather her inner strength, and catch up with her magazine consumption. In this instance, she was engrossed in the glossy pages of *Jen*, a monthly mixture of fashion, celebrity, and real-life problems Alison had avidly lapped up since she was a preteen.

The thunder of boots on creaking floorboards ended her alone time with *Jen*. In they charged, standard-issue henchmen, nothing she hadn't seen before. Six of them. Big, bald guys, tree-trunk forearms, colossal chests, the usual tattoos. Except for one glowering dude, who had a map of Belgium inked across his *whole face* (unless it was a birthmark, in which case Alison knew the *perfect* dermatologist who could clear him right up . . .).

The hulking underlings surrounded her, moving ever closer in a tightening circle. Close enough for them to see their huge, hairless domes reflected in her dark glasses. After a moment of enigmatic silence, Alison looked up from the pages of *Jen*.

"A good magazine is like a good friend," she said, as if addressing a group of acquaintances. "You look forward to hanging out with her every month. You can't wait to find out what she's wearing, see what she's done with her hair, and catch up with all the latest gossip."

The circle of brutal henchmen regarded Alison with confusion. They were a pretty fearsome collection of hombres, but she didn't seem the slightest bit scared. Even more bizarrely, she seemed to assume they would be interested in listening to her babble about her magazine.

"But that makes her sound superficial and there's *so* much more to her than that," Alison continued. "She's the kind of friend who wants to see you shine. And she really wants you to have every opportunity to be as awesome as she is." To illustrate her point, Alison brandished the cover of *Jen*. Treasure Spinney, beloved star of the long-running teen TV drama *Signal Hill*, smiled her dazzling multimillion-dollar smile and pointed a finger at the readers of America. The headline asked, "Are You America's No. 1 *Jen* Girl?"

"Every year, we choose from a pool of smart, talented girls to come and intern for us," recited Alison from memory. "But this year, we're holding an extra-special place for an extra-special girl. This year, we're looking for the reader who sums up everything *Jen* is about. Send us an essay or a video that lets us see exactly why you're America's No. 1 *Jen* Girl, and you can spend the spring interning at *Jen*!" Alison stared at the henchmen, willing them to share her excitement. "Come on! Working at *Jen*? Total dream job!"

They remained mute and scowling with no more life to them than the rusted metal girders that framed the empty, dust-filled warehouse. She wouldn't accept their lack of response.

"You're telling me you don't think that new editor's a genius? She's *fifteen*, for God's sake! Okay, when I heard the owner's daughter was taking charge, I was *septical*."

A couple of the brutal henchmen swapped baffled glances. Did the babbling girl mean *skeptical*? Was she deliberately mangling the language?

Alison continued, her enthusiasm growing. "But she's *totally* turned *Jen* around. Her ideas are amazing. I'm obsessed with the What's Hot and What's Not List. It's always so right on about what's in and what's out. The minute they're over a celeb or a trend—*bang*: career *ovah*! It's the first thing I turn to every month. Don't tell me you don't do the same when the new issue of *Henchman Monthly* comes out!"

Alison glanced around the warehouse. For the first time, the visible portion of her face appeared to show signs of consternation. "Oh, no!" she gasped. "I'm not the first one here, am I?" Her voice grew shrill. "Tell me I didn't show up to the entire wrong place? Tell me this is where they're holding the America's No. 1 *Jen* Girl launch party?"

The henchmen began to grin at her distress. Little girl lost.

As rapidly as she seemed to fall apart, Alison began to brighten. "I'm so stupid. The party's *downstairs*. Where you're hiding Treasure Spinney." With that, she pointed both of her Chanel Vendetta–tipped index fingers at the ground and began to spin in a graceful pirouette. As she whirled, flames shot out of her fingers and quickly burned a hole into the ground.

The unexpected combination of the spinning and the flames froze the six men. They continued to stand, staring, as Alison wiggled her fingers in a goodbye gesture and dropped through the hole. *Messing with henchmen*, she thought as she fell. *Never gets old.*

I've been here too long. I've started to hallucinate, thought Heather Harker as the ceiling of her cell seemed to open up and a girl in dark glasses and a thick gold chain fell on top of her.

"It's okay, Treasure. I'm gonna get you out of this," yelled Alison as she plummeted through the hole and hit the bed. Then she got a look at the terrified face of the fourteen-year-old girl whose body and lumpy bed she was lying on top of. The skin was flawless, the features were angelic, the hair tumbled into chestnut curls. All the trademarks of the tiny TV queen. The chic-but-quirky ensemble—black lace Forever 21 top, gold Miu Miu skirt, Givenchy wedges—was something Treasure's stylists would put together for her. But on closer examination—and it was difficult to get much closer than Alison currently was—there was something . . . *missing*. A further second ticked by, and then Alison knew what the girl was lacking. Charisma. Whatever the quality was that differentiated celebrities from civilians, this girl didn't possess so much as an ounce of it.

"You're not Treasure Spinney!" said Alison accusingly.

"That's what I've been trying to tell them!" moaned the girl. "I'm her stand-in. I do the stuff she doesn't want to do. Like show up for rehearsals or wave to fans or go to the launch of the *Jen* Girl contest. I kept saying, 'You've made a mistake. I'm not Treasure, I'm Heather Harker.' But they wouldn't listen. They grabbed me after the *Jen* Girl rehearsal. They threw me in a van, and then they locked me in here."

Alison looked at the tear-stained girl and felt a stab of

sympathy. You spend your days standing in the shadow of a star. You're invisible the second she shows up. And then you get abducted by inept Belgians!

"Who are *you*?" Heather Harker suddenly demanded.

Alison paused. What should she tell the girl? That less than six months ago she was the privileged and popular daughter of a Brentwood attorney? That her best friends were so insecure and jealous of what they perceived as her perfect life that they manipulated her into undergoing experimental cosmetic surgery? That the operation went haywire, turning her into a freak whose fingers burst into flames every time her emotions were aroused? That her fire-starting abilities were ignited by a run-in with the *real* Treasure Spinney when they fought over a sale item at Barneys? That she had taken what some might see as a disability and used it to her advantage? That her stepmother, Carmen, had turned out to be a criminally insane mind controller who almost succeeded in throwing Alison's father off a museum roof? That Alison had crushed Carmen under a giant ball of frozen poo? That she led a double existence as beloved Beverly Hills High School student Alison Cole by day and superhero Hottie by night (or, technically, by late afternoon to early evening because she still had homework and a social life)?

There wasn't time to tell her any of that, and, besides, Heather looked so freaked out Alison doubted she could comprehend any of it. So she said, "I'm an angel."

Heather's eyes widened. Her mouth grew slack.

Alison pointed up at the hole in the ceiling. "I knew you were in need. So I came to help you. That's what we do." *I hope she's buying this*, thought Alison. The dazed look on Heather's face indicated that she needed to attribute the bizarre things that were happening to *something*. It might as well be divine intervention. "If I'm going to get us out of here, I need you to do one thing for me," Alison went on.

"Anything," breathed Heather, who had made the instant leap from sniveling stand-in to full-on believer in all things angelic.

"I need you to close your eyes and pray. And don't open them until something miraculous happens."

Heather didn't need telling twice. She rolled off the bed, nudged the tin plate containing a half-eaten Belgian waffle to one side, squeezed her eyes shut, pushed her palms together, and began moving her lips in silent prayer. Alison looked at the girl and experienced brief but bitter pangs of disappointment that it wasn't the *real* Treasure Spinney on her knees praying for salvation. Then she snapped out of it. She was a superhero who fought for the unprotected and the oppressed, and, clearly, few people were more oppressed than Treasure Spinney's stand-in.

Alison kicked out hard, shoving the bed across the cell. Then she pointed her fingers at the ceiling. Six faces, one bearing a tattoo of Belgium, stared down in amazement. Alison burned a bigger hole. The six faces started screaming as the floor gave way beneath their feet. She jumped up and pulled Heather to her feet as the wailing henchmen fell through the floor and landed on the cold, hard concrete.

"That's the power of prayer," Alison said. Stepping over the stunned, twitching bodies, she shot out a hand and melted the bars of the cell. "Let's go," Alison ordered the frazzled stand-in, grabbing her arm and pulling her from the cell. The pair picked up speed as they fled the maze of cells in the basement of the warehouse and charged toward an emergency exit. The door opened.

"Is that another angel?" gasped Heather.

Alison's heart started beating faster. It was her boyfriend, Tommy Hull, universally known as T, Beverly Hills High's Junior Class President of Cuteness. Once he had regarded her superpowers with something approaching revulsion, but now they fought evil and injustice side by side.

Alison looked at him, standing in the doorway, a total rock star in his black leather jacket, white T-shirt, and distressed jeans. "I don't know if I'm ready for a relationship," she'd told him some months earlier. And she'd meant it when she'd said it. She'd done the research, and the research had proved conclusively: You could have superpowers or you could have a rich and satisfying dating life. You could not have both. *But,* Alison remembered arguing with herself, *he's unbelievably supportive of you being a superhero, you've still got a big fat crush on him, and if you keep acting like you only wanna be friends, some sixteen-year-old is gonna snap him up. And Q: How much will you love that? A: Not very.* Alison quickly decided that *other* superheroes were welcome to live lonely lives filled with self-sacrifice, but she wasn't about to let a hot, devoted guy go to waste. So now they fought evil together. And bought little surprise gifts for each other. And drove out to Malibu on weekends. And took long walks on Paradise Cove. And made whispered promises that they would always be there for each other.

"No," Alison told Heather, who was staring at T with an expression that could only be described as worshipful. "That's my boyfriend."

Alison and T gazed warmly at each other. The flush of first love still lingered.

Then a thick, hairy tattooed arm wrapped itself around T's throat, lifting him off his feet.

"*T!*" screamed Alison. Before she could rush to her boy-friend's aid, a *new* group of henchmen, this one armed to the teeth, charged into the basement. Alison looked at the oncoming horde. Then she looked back at T, who was struggling with a muscled opponent on the steps leading up to the emergency exit.

"I'm on this," gasped T, swinging a powerful elbow into his attacker's jaw. "You get her out of here!"

Alison threw her arms wide open. A wall of fire suddenly separated her from the rampaging henchmen. Heather uttered a gurgle of fear and disbelief. "Are you *sure* you're an angel?" she managed to ask.

"Why? Don't I seem angelic?" demanded Alison as she yanked hard on the girl's arm and dragged her away from the flames.

Minutes later, Alison, Heather, and a bruised, banged-up but unbeaten T made their way through the emergency exit down to the lower-level parking garage. It was deserted, apart from the burned-out, rusty shells of some ancient expired automobiles.

Alison smiled at Heather. "Don't worry. You'll be back pretending to be Treasure Spinney before you know it."

Heather's mouth twitched. From her reaction, she looked as if she was about to confess how she *really* felt about her day job. Then five figures descended from the ceiling, landing on the roofs of the cars. Alison and T stared at their unexpected new adversaries. They were clad in head-to-toe black. Even their faces were swathed in dark cloth. They were soundless. They moved with a deadly grace. They were like panthers.

"Ninjas," breathed Alison. "Belgian ninjas."

T stood by her side. "Nothing you can't handle," he said supportively. She wasn't so sure. These weren't steroid freaks with maps on their faces. These were lethal assassins who floated on the wind and laughed at gravity.

"Yo, Hottie," called a voice from behind a nearby concrete pillar. Alison didn't turn around. She didn't have to. She knew who it was. David Eels. Her superhero sidekick. The guy who first encouraged her to explore her powers. The guy who told her how special she could be. The guy who named her Hottie. The guy who fell victim to an unrequited crush that momentarily capsized their friendship. And, finally, the guy who was her rock-solid right hand. David might not be blessed with T's looks or build or height or athleticism or ability to make the female heart go boom-boom-boom, but there would be no Hottie without him.

"One thing we never covered during our extensive superhero training sessions," said David.

"What's that?"

"Gadgets."

From his position behind the pillar, David tossed an object into Alison's open palm. She looked down at her hand. She was holding something round and metal with a wire wound around the center.

"It's a yo-yo," noted T.

"Hence the 'Yo, Hottie' greeting," explained David.

Alison stared at the yo-yo in her hand. It was bedazzled and had the *H* logo on both sides. For a second, she didn't get it. Then she saw the shadows of the ninjas as they moved like leaves in the breeze. And then she got it. Alison couldn't move like the ninjas. She couldn't fight like them. But David had just given her something that made her their equal. He'd given her a yo-yo that in her hands became . . . *a ball of fire.* She tried a couple of practice swings.

"Let that little guy fly!" demanded David. "It's solid steel. It can take up to twenty-five hundred degrees."

Alison watched the way the bedazzled yo-yo sent colors shimmering across the dark garage. Then, without warning, she lashed out her wrist, sending fire streaming down the wire and causing the yo-yo to burst into flames. Striding confidently out of the shadows and into the middle of the warehouse, she swung the blazing yo-yo above her head like a lasso.

A ninja leapt from the roof of a rusted Pinto. Alison swung low and struck her attacker smack on the kneecap. The ninja let out a muffled groan from beneath his mask. He swayed for a second, then slumped to the ground. David and T saw the next ninja bound high into the air and fall silently, dropping from the ceiling, ready to engulf Alison like a deadly black cloud.

"Above you!" they screamed in unison.

Alison dropped to her knees, leaned back, and threw the yo-yo straight up, smashing into the lower part of the ninja's swathed head. Then she sprang to her feet and stepped aside so the ninja fell face-first onto the ground. Groaning, he pulled down the folds of the mask to spit out a pair of broken teeth.

"*Ma teef,*" he whined.

"*Thorry,*" snickered Alison.

Two more black-clad assassins sprang at Alison. She swung the fiery yo-yo in an arcing motion. As it sailed downward, it set the first ninja's foot on fire, leaving him hopping and flailing. On its return journey, it clattered off the second attacker's ear, causing him to howl in pain and frantically unravel the mask as the flames spread. Alison reeled the yo-yo back in and gazed at it affectionately.

"Loving the gadget," she said to David as he walked out from behind the pillar.

T and David nodded at each other. They weren't exactly friends. But they maintained a cautious mutual respect.

David was about to introduce himself to Heather, but before he could speak, she was yanked off the ground and up into the air. The last ninja! Alison, David, and T stared in horror as the screaming stand-in was hoisted skyward on what seemed like invisible strings. Alison shot the burning yo-yo up into the air.

"Kick out!" she shouted to Heather. "High as you can!" The yo-yo soared toward the ceiling, following the ninja and his petrified captive. Heather heard Alison's command. She kicked both legs up past her head. The yo-yo slammed straight into the ninja's crotch, setting it alight. From beneath the mask came a pained, high-pitched moan. David and T both winced in silent empathy. Then the ninja let go of Heather. David and T ran to the nearest car and dragged out the seats.

Heather continued screaming as she saw the ground rushing to meet her. With amazing timing, David and T managed to position the seats at the exact spot where they would cushion her fall. Heather collapsed into the car seat, spraying foam stuffing all over the garage. For a moment, she was still and silent. Then she gasped, "I hate Treasure Spinney. Being her stand-in is the worst job in the world. She's mean and spoiled, and she doesn't care about anyone else. I wish it had been her that got kidnapped!"

T and David looked mystified. Then they both said, "Stand-in?"

David looked outraged. "We wasted the gadget on a stand-in?"

Alison was about to explain Heather's circumstances when a harsh, Belgian-accented voice echoed around the garage.

"Step away from the star!"

Alison, David, and T looked up and saw Heather's kidnapper. The kingpin who had masterminded the entire abduction was walking toward them, gun in hand.

"Nice hair," remarked Alison of the crime boss's well-kept mane.

The kingpin acknowledged the compliment. "Nice hands," he said to Alison. "But I bet I can put at least one bullet into at least one of your boyfriends before you get to me."

Alison was about to explain that only one of the boys was actually her boyfriend. But then she worried that David might be a little sensitive about the way things had turned out. He never said anything, but she sometimes thought she saw a wistful look in his eyes.

With a wave of his gun, the crime boss gestured for Alison, David, and T to move away from Heather.

David shook his head scornfully at the villain. "You're not in Antwerp anymore, buddy. This is the USA. We expect a certain degree of ingenuity from our criminal masterminds. Snatching a stand-in on your first big job is not gonna do wonders for your reputation."

The kingpin's face clouded. A brief burst of uncertainty. *Stand-in?* David saw the moment of weakness. "Blast him," he yelled at Alison. "He's not gonna shoot us."

"Yes, he is," said the kingpin, suddenly aware he had nothing left to lose. The crime boss took aim straight between T's eyes. He got ready to pull the trigger.

Alison pointed her fingers directly at the kingpin's face. Could she get him before he got T? *I hate standoffs*, she thought bitterly.

Alison and the kingpin remained locked in the same position. Neither wavering in their intent. Then a hand snuck up behind the crime boss's head and, with one deft tug, yanked the wig off, revealing the bare skin beneath.

"*Ewww*," moaned a female voice.

"More *eeews* than anyone has ever *ewwww*ed before!" replied a second female voice.

Alison beamed with joy. "Hey, sexy ladies," she called out.

Running away from the horrified kingpin, who was covering his exposed baldness with both hands, were Alison's two BFFs. As they scampered across the garage, Kellyn Levy tossed the wig to Dorinda Galen. The freaked-out Belgian crime boss probably thought his toupee had been abducted by two more members of Alison's team. He wasn't to know that the blisteringly cynical Kellyn used to despise being perceived as Alison's sidekick. Or that Dorinda had been so fearful of being rendered invisible by Alison's popularity that she had passed herself off as French for three years. Their relationship had been fraught with petty jealousies and disharmony, but at this moment, Alison looked at the two girls who had caused her so much grief with nothing but love and affection.

"Take the hair," yelled the pale, sharp-featured Kellyn, lobbing the wig to Dorinda.

"It's like a dead cat. You take it," squealed the buxom, exotic Dorinda, throwing it back.

Grossed out by their proximity to the crime boss's wig, Kellyn tossed the hairpiece back to its owner. The kingpin caught the fake hair as it flew across the garage. As he snatched it and went to position it back on his head, Alison opened fire. The wig returned to the kingpin's head at the exact second she set it alight. His screams echoed across the building.

"What a hothead!" said Alison, David, and T in unison. They looked at each other in amazement. Their quips had become synchronized.

"We're such a team!" marveled Alison.

"We're the Department of Hotness," pronounced David.

"'*The Department of Hotness*,'" repeated an awed Alison. "*Loving that.*"

The wail of distant sirens increased in volume. The LAPD was on its way. When the cops arrived, they'd find one fried kingpin, five limping ninjas, and a bunch of beaten-up, bald henchmen. All trussed up and waiting to be hauled off. What they wouldn't find was the Department of Hotness.

Just before Alison prepared to leave the scene of the crime, she turned to Heather Harker. The stand-in's face was scarlet.

Her makeup was smeared across her eyes and mouth. Her hair was wild. She was still visibly shaken up. "You gonna be okay?" asked Alison.

Heather gazed into Alison's eyes. "You're not really an angel, are you?"

The girl's disbelief annoyed Alison. "Sorry if that ruined the whole rescue thing for you."

"It didn't," said Heather. "But can you tell me who you are? So I know who I'm thanking."

"I go by Hottie. But that stays a little secret between us, okay?"

Heather ran a finger across her lips and mimed turning a key in a lock. Then she mimed putting the key back in the lock and turning it counterclockwise. "Oh, and that stuff I said about Treasure? I didn't really mean it. She's under a lot of pressure with the show and everything. She's not so bad."

"I hope she appreciates all you do for her," said Alison.

"*That* really would be a miracle." Heather grinned.

Alison smiled at the stand-in one last time, then hurried to join her friends.

Alison, David, Kellyn, Dorinda, and T strode in perfect precision to the Mercedes, where their driver, the unkempt, heavyset, nineteen-year-old college dropout known as Designated Dean, waited to whisk them away from the crime scene.

"That was *classic*," babbled a hyper David. "A classic mission. A classic *mish*!"

"That was a nonstop roller coaster of action," agreed T.

"That was just another episode in the legendary adventures of the Department of Hotness," said Alison, who then pointed a fiery finger at Designated Dean. "Now play my song, Double D!"

Designated Dean cranked up the sound system. A crunching wall of guitars and thudding drums roared out followed by a constipated-sounding singer screeching about being back in black.

"That's not my song!" complained Alison. "My song's 'Betcha Wish Your Girlfriend Was Hot Like Me!'"

Designated Dean shook his head. "Driver picks the tunes. And there's only two kinds of music: AC or DC."

Alison found herself bobbing her head in time to the deafening rock classic. David, T, Dorinda, and Kellyn were doing the same. "I like them both," she said and climbed aboard the powder blue Mercedes, which, during times of superhero duty, was known as the Hottiemobile.

The car roared away from the abandoned warehouse seconds before the LAPD arrived. Alison sat in the front passenger seat, glowing with satisfaction and excitement. She looked around her. At T. At David. At Kellyn and Dorinda and even Double D. They were an amazing, instinctual, fearless, fantastic crime-fighting unit, and she'd never been so proud to call them her friends.

Nothing can break us apart, she thought.

TWO
Things Fall Apart

Alison checked her watch. It was four in the afternoon. What were other LA girls doing? Making out with boys. Playing soccer. Adding friends to and removing over-sharing losers from their Facebooks. Shopping. Tanning. Twittering. Putting together personalized playlists for their iPhones. Changing their hair color. Practicing yoga. Accessorizing their dogs. Bidding for vintage shoes on eBay. Spreading cruel rumors about their enemies. Rehearsing dance routines. The options were endless. And what was she—probably the only, certainly the cutest superhero in Los Angeles—doing? She was standing inside a cardboard packing crate used to transport refrigerators.

The caliber of missions calling for the skills of the Department of Hotness had definitely peaked after the incident with Treasure Spinney's stand-in. Subsequent weeks had seen them bring a bad babysitter to justice, stop a lazy dog walker outsourcing his clients to skateboard crews, and track down the notorious garden-gnome thief of Los Feliz (who, disappointingly, turned out to be a guy who stole ornaments from backyards and not, as the Department of Hotness had hoped, a garden gnome with criminal tendencies).

And now it was four-oh-one in the afternoon, and Alison was in a big box at the back of the branch of the Nordstrom department store situated at The Grove, LA's upmarket wonderland of a shopping mall. How she wished she could be store-hopping and celeb-spotting like all the other gawkers in the Grove. But plans had been made. It had been decided that being in the big box would add the element of surprise needed to end the reign of terror perpetrated by the PBG.

Alison remembered clicking on the link to the clip David had sent her some days earlier. She recalled squinting at the shaky footage. A lone girl walking into view. Looking around nervously. Calling out, "Hello? I'm here for the party." The sudden emergence of three more girls. All wearing hats. All carrying bags. Opening their bags together. Pulling out balloons. Hurling the balloons at the shocked girl. Dousing her from head to toe. Screaming, "Welcome to the pee party," and then running off, still howling with laughter. Leaving the girl soaked and sobbing.

"PBG? Pottery Barn Group? I'm very much hoping," Alison remembered asking.

"The PBG," David had explained, "The Pee Balloon Girls." A clique of Beverly Hills High freshmen who had candidly assessed their looks, personalities, and talents. A clique who had then decided the only way they were ever going to be popular, famous, or, in any way noticed was to befriend losers even more pathetic than they were, lure them to secluded spots, and drench them in pee. Although they had only managed to lure a couple of hapless victims, their reputation had spread like a billowing pee stain and their name was whispered with fear. "This looks like the next mish for the Department of Hotness," David had said.

Alison remembered her outrage at the clip, at the very *notion* that such an abomination as the PBG should be allowed to exist at *her* school. But now it was four-oh-eight, and she was still in the big box, peering at the wonders of the Grove through a line of dime-size breathing holes. At least she had *Jen* to keep her company. With some difficulty, Alison angled herself so that the four dime-size shafts of light fell onto the glossy pages of her favorite magazine. Soon she was immersed in the contents. Time flew by as she flicked through *What's In Your Bag? Sidewalk Supermodels*, and the regular letter from Pixie Furmanovsky, the preternaturally talented fifteen-year-old editor.

"I wish I could work with her," Alison sighed to herself. The moment the wish left her lips, Alison turned to the page filled with details about the America's No. 1 *Jen* Girl contest. She inhaled sharply. When Alison first became aware of the contest, her immediate response was *Yes! I am America's No. 1 Jen Girl!* But being a superhero had been her priority. Now, standing in the big gloomy box, she was starting to wonder if she hadn't got her priorities wrong.

Her iPhone emitted its receiving blip. She clicked a fingernail on the *Mail* icon. David had sent her a sound file. Another click.

After a second, the sound of pounding drums blared tinnily from the phone. Dramatic strings sawed over the drums. Then a horn section blasted, honking in triumph. "What am I listening to?" Alison wondered aloud. Her phone beeped. David's goofily grinning face filled the screen. *What a waste that he gets to hang out in the mall waiting for the mish to begin while I'm stuck in the big box*, she mourned. *It ought to be the other way around.*

"You like?" he asked.

"Like what?" she retorted. "Being in the big box or listening to this mental marching-band music you sent me?"

"Both," said David, "but especially the latter. It's your theme."

"My what? . . ." said Alison, confused.

"Something else no self-respecting superhero should be without," he said proudly. "Her own theme. Makes her entrance that much more dramatic. Builds anticipation for what's to come. Makes her ultimate victory that much more exciting. Leaves the world waiting breathlessly for her next appearance." David let a moment pass before saying. "By *her*, I meant *your*. You got that, right? It's your own personalized superhero theme."

Alison paused to fully process the information that David was excitedly imparting. "You wrote me a theme?" she asked.

"I did it on GarageBand. Easy-peasy for someone of my outstanding abilities," he said. "I just thought AC/DC's cool and everything, but you need your own sound track. . . ."

"*David*," said Alison softly. "First the gadget, now my own theme . . ." She was touched. "You are an awesome friend. I just wish I was a better superhero."

David was quick to allay her insecurities. "You still rule. It's not your fault the caliber of missions has deteriorated. It'll pick up again. Evil doesn't take a vacation. And if it does, it only goes to Vegas for the weekend and then comes back stronger than ever."

Alison laughed. It was so weird that they'd ended up being best friends, but she couldn't imagine letting a day go by without talking to him.

"I promise you won't have to spend another afternoon bored inside a big box," he declared.

"I'm not *that* bored," she said. "I've got *Jen* with me."

"Which takes care of both reading and your toilet paper needs" was David's immediate and entirely sincere reaction.

Alison scowled. As close as they were, David continued to be more enamored with Alison's alter ego than he was with her everyday life as an ordinary—albeit immeasurably popular—teenager. David wasn't kidding when he mocked her devotion to *Jen*. She hated it when he dismissed it as a "BIP handbook." BIP, his acronym for *Because I'm Pretty*, was the most scathing insult in his arsenal, and if he didn't understand her devotion to her favorite magazine, it made her feel like he really didn't understand her.

"Sorry," she said. "Why don't you write me up a list of all the comic books you think I should be reading?"

"I'll do that," he promised.

"A big long list."

"I'm already on it."

"And then shove it up your butt."

David laughed for a few seconds. Then the laughter stopped. "Time to plug your brain back in," he said, suddenly all urgency. "Mish *on*!"

Alison ended the call and took up position at the four

breathing holes. The PBG target du jour wandered toward the back of the store. The thick glasses. The prominent front teeth. The nervous habit of tugging at the ends of her hair. *Victim much?*

Through the holes in the big box, Alison could see the anticipation on the girl's face. *I'm meeting my cool new friends here. They're taking me to a party. Finally, I'm going to be accepted.* Then she could see the doubt trickle in. *But why did they want to meet me at the back of a store where there's no one else around?* Finally, relief, as the girl's cool new friends appeared. Four of them. All wearing Burberry bucket hats pulled down to obscure their eyes. All wearing Cavalli silver gladiator sandals. All wearing Juicy Couture silk-chiffon ruffle-front blouses. All carrying fake Chanel bags. And all saying nothing. Just staring at the dish of the day. The dish they were about to devour.

"*Pliss. Is right place, yis? For pyarty?*" asked the girl in a quavery Eastern European accent.

"*Yis, little Russian nobody. Is right place,*" mocked the members of the PBG.

Acting in unison, the four angels of darkness opened their bags and pulled out balloons. "Welcome to the pee party!" they chorused. "Let's turn this White Russian green!"

Suddenly, the terrified girl's BlackBerry Storm played the opening notes of Tchaikovsky's "1812 Overture." She raised a finger, gesturing to the PBG to pause their assault.

"*Yis?*" said the girl into her phone. She nodded, then held the phone up to the PBG. "*Is for you.*"

The members of the PBG looked at each other. This wasn't supposed to happen.

"Hi girls. I got something I'm just *bursting* to show you," said the voice from the phone. From inside her hiding place, Alison clicked off her phone and poked a finger through a hole in the big box. Then four things happened. Or one thing happened four times.

Pop! The first balloon burst, soaking the first PBG's gladiator sandals in pee.

Pop! The second balloon burst, soaking the second PBG's silk-chiffon blouse in pee.

Pop! The third balloon burst, soaking the third PBG's Burberry hat in pee. (She foolishly tried to cover her face while still clutching the balloon.)

Pop! The fourth PBG was so scared, she burst her own pee balloon.

The quartet of sodden tormentors was almost catatonic with fear. They had no idea what had just happened. They had no idea what would happen next. What happened next was that the big cardboard box at the back of the department store suddenly burst into flames and a girl emerged, wearing huge dark glasses and a chain that ended in a big gold *H*.

Alison paused briefly to savor the impact of her entrance. The members of the PBG were weeping and clinging to each other.

And that's *why they call me Hottie*, she thought smugly.

"Smile pretty for the cameras, girls," commanded Alison as she went to take her place at the side of the now not-at-all-scared Russian girl.

The pair was joined by three masked figures carrying camera phones, documenting the PBG in all their soggy shame. When the job involved saving Belgians, only Alison needed to don her disguise. But when taking down BHHS students who could potentially recognize them, the Department had to remain anonymous. So T was invisible underneath a motorcycle helmet. David wore a Mexican wrestling mask, and only dark glasses were detectable under the hood of Kellyn's sweatshirt. The presence of the Department of Hotness caused the PBG to snivel and whimper some more. Alison let them stew for a few more seconds. Then she addressed them.

"Are you evil little twits proud of yourselves?"

The PBG remained locked in a tight, tearful huddle. They barely understood the question.

"Um . . . yes?" one of them volunteered.

"Wrong answer. Horribly wrong. You should be ashamed. Think about who you are. Think about what you're doing."

Kellyn stifled a yawn. She sensed a superhero morality speech on the horizon.

David nudged her and muttered, "Shut up," from beneath his mask.

"Sorry," sneered Kellyn from inside her hood. "I forgot you have to hang on her every word. What do you do? Scribble it all down in a little book? Sleep with it under your pillow at night? Is it almost like having her right there with you? *Awww*."

"Leave him alone," murmured the Russian girl to no one in particular.

Alison shot a sidelong glance at Kellyn and David. This was her big superhero morality speech. They weren't supposed to be talking. She carried on. "You dress up in disguises. You lure strangers to secluded spots, and you soak them in pee and film them. Does that make you feel good about yourselves? *Does it?*"

The PBG Who Always Said *Um* spoke up. "Um . . . *you* dress up in disguises. *You* lured us to a secluded spot. *You* soaked us in pee, and *you* filmed us."

Kellyn burst out laughing.

David snarled, "Shut *up*."

"It's true, though," Kellyn said.

"It's clearly different," retorted Alison.

"Um . . . how's it different?" asked The Um Girl, who, it was becoming clear, was the most articulate member of the PBG.

"Because I'm teaching you the difference between right and wrong," said an exasperated Alison.

"Um. . . so it's right when you do it, but it's wrong when we do it?"

"I don't even know if it's wrong when *you* guys do it," remarked Kellyn.

Alison stared at her, openmouthed.

"Seriously, though," Kellyn continued, "I can think of a whole lot of people who could benefit from a good pee bath. Pointing no fingers," she said, while pointing straight at David.

"Stop," murmured the Russian girl.

The PBG began to giggle and relax.

"So go join the PBG then—if you think they're so awesome," said David. "We won't miss you."

"Oh, but I'll miss you, Eels," mocked Kellyn.

"Don't tell them my *name*," seethed a shocked David.

"Yeah, like any of them know who you are. Any of you girls know a David Eels?"

"Um. . . I know a David Bales. He's kind of cute."

"So's David Eels," murmured the Russian girl to herself.

Alison couldn't believe this. She had totally lost control of the mish. Kellyn was *completely* undermining her, while the real enemy stood by and laughed. She had to regain control of the situation. Alison pointed her fingers and, in four short, speedy blasts, burned the bucket hats off the heads of the PBG. The terror-stricken freshmen cried and clung to each other anew.

Alison pointed at their flushed, naked faces. "Which one of you is the leader?"

No one spoke.

"Is it you, Infected Nose Ring?"

The PBG whose nose ring had spread an infection remained mute.

"How about you, Pink Glitter Eye Shadow?"

The PBG who had slathered on an over-generous amount of MAC eye pigment said nothing.

"Okay." Alison shrugged, turning to the tangerine-colored PBG. "We'll say it's you, Too Long in the Tanning Booth. I hear one word—*one*—that you're still in the pee business and I'm coming after you. And don't think I won't hear about it. I've got ears everywhere."

"That's why she never wears a bikini," interrupted Kellyn.

The PBG broke into shrill laughter. Alison and David stared at Kellyn, who gave them an apologetic I-couldn't-stop-myself grin.

And then T started walking toward the PBG.

I have never loved anyone more than I love you right this minute, thought Alison. She knew T had her back. She knew he'd never let her down. He could see that she was in danger of losing control of the situation, and there he was, about to bring the PBG to heel with his natural authority. And then T pushed past the pee girls and kept walking. Didn't look back. Didn't say a word. Didn't take off his helmet. Just walked away. Alison stared after him. She was about to call his name. Then she remembered their identities were supposed to be secret. Alison kept her eyes on T's quickly dwindling figure. *He can't just be walking away. He must be coming back.* But he didn't seem to be coming back. He seemed to be walking away. And then Kellyn made some crack about T having a bladder infection. David told her to shut up, and the PBG broke out in high-pitched giggles. Suddenly, fighting evil was the last thing Alison wanted to do. Standing at the back of Nordstrom was the last place she wanted to be. She pointed a warning finger at the PBG. The high-pitched giggling stopped.

"Know what I've been doing here?" she asked briskly.

The PBG stayed silent.

"Going easy on you is what I've been doing," said Alison. "If there's a next time, I'm turning up the heat, *and you don't want me to turn up the heat!*"

With that, Alison stalked away. The PBG girls stared after her, awestruck. "Um . . . we're sorry," The Um Girl called after her.

"We won't do it again," promised Infected Nose Ring.

Kellyn, David, and the Russian girl stared after the departing Alison. *What was* that *about?* David pulled out his phone and played the *Hottie* theme. Alison didn't turn around. Being a superhero was the last thing on her mind.

THREE
Love is a Battlefield

After most mishes, Alison made a point of immediately stuffing her dark wig and gold chain into a back-pack. But T's unexpected exit reordered her priorities. With the big gold chain banging painfully off her hip, she trotted toward the Fairfax Farmer's Market, situated adjacent to the Grove.

T was already at his parking spot and opening the door of his Chevy Impala.

"Hey," said Alison, catching up to him. "Everything okay?"

T hung by the door. "Sure," he said, sounding like a guy who was not in the mood to utter anything more than monosyllables.

"You walked away. In the middle of the mish. You walked away. You didn't say anything. Are you okay? Do you feel sick?

Is it something to do with your bladder? There was a lot of pee around."

"I'm fine," he muttered, still not meeting her eyes.

"You're not, though," said Alison, pushing. "You walked away. Without a word. You never do that. You always have my back. So, why?"

"It's all just so . . . disorganized," said T, finally looking straight at her. "It's just a bunch of kids shouting at each other."

Alison nodded. "It's Kellyn. She's an underminer. We can talk to her at the Koo Koo Roo."

The thought of the ritual post-mish dinner at Alison's favorite poultry chain didn't seem to fill T with excitement. "Do I have to go?" He sighed.

Alison pulled off her dark glasses and stared at her boyfriend. "You don't *have* to go. I don't want to *force* you to go. But it's something I'd think you'd *want* to do."

"I mean, if it was just you and me . . ." muttered T.

"It is just you and me. And David and Kel. And Dor. The Department of Hotness."

T rubbed the space between his eyebrows. He *so* did not want to be having this conversation. All around him, happy couples wandered hand in hand. None of them seemed to have any problem communicating. "I just think you guys would have more fun hanging out together," he said. "You're all the same age."

Alison felt the rush of heat at her fingertips. She took a breath and attempted to rein in her temper. "That's true," she said, trying to remain calm. "You are certainly older and more mature than myself and my friends. I didn't realize it was such a strain for you to be around me when you could be discussing politics and the state of the onion with all these geniuses that I've been keeping you from."

T reached for Alison's hand. "That came out wrong "

"Oh?" she snapped, pulling her hand away. "It sounded different in your head all the times you were thinking about how much you hated hanging out with me?"

"I never thought that!" he protested.

"Well, you don't have to worry about it anymore! Congratulations!"

T stood unhappily by his car watching his girlfriend walking quickly and angrily away, her gold chain banging painfully off her hip.

At that moment, David and Kellyn exited the elevator at Level Six of the Grove's vast parking garage. Their disguises were gone, but their bickering was still very much in evidence.

"God, Eels, when was the last time you took a shower?" barked Kellyn.

"I don't know," replied David. "Let me check with your mother. She was there at the time."

"Vomiting profusely," sneered Kellyn.

"Like she did when the nurse said, 'It's a girl'?"

"No, Eels, we're talking about my mother, not yours."

The Russian girl with the buckteeth and the glasses followed them. Kellyn glanced back at her. "I think you can dispense with the Oscar-winning disguise now, Meryl Sheep."

Dorinda started to remove the fake front teeth.

"Ah, leave 'em in." David smiled. "You look cute."

Dorinda, entirely unused to receiving compliments or attention, flushed and stared at the ground.

"Fine," said Kellyn. "You stay in disguise. Eels, you take off your hideous mask."

"It is kind of grotesque," agreed David. "But then, I did model it after you."

Kellyn pretended to pull an arrow out of her heart.

As they headed toward the Hottiemobile, David turned back to Dorinda. "The reviews are in: the accents, the personalities, the way you put yourself in the line of danger—Department of Hotness MVP. You were the cherry at the top of the superhero sundae today."

"That's funny," said Kellyn. "I thought Eels was the cherry."

David and Kellyn continued taking shots at each other. As far as Dorinda was concerned, they could have been clicking like Zulu tribesmen. After a lifetime of feeling invisible—of believing herself to be *lesser* because she lacked Alison's blonde beauty and Kellyn's piercing wit—someone had called her cute. More than that, he had called *her* the MVP. And once David had called her that, Dorinda had stopped hearing anything else.

Making her way back to the Grove, Alison played the unexpected fight with T over and over in her head. *You're all the same age.* That's what he'd said. *He thinks I'm immature!* She couldn't believe it. *I'm the most mature person I know!* And then a voice interrupted her thoughts. A bright, cheerful, almost-musical voice calling out her name. Alison turned to see the source of the voice. It was Lark Rise, the willowy junior who had managed T's class president campaign, rushing out of Anthropologie and heading toward her.

Alison admired Lark's tireless drive and dedication. Name the after-school activity, Lark was part of it. Name the worthy cause, Lark was collecting donations for it. But Alison couldn't escape the feeling that Lark Rise looked down on her a little bit.

"Look at you, you pretty little thing," cooed Lark. "Always so well put together. And look at me." She rolled her eyes in a self-deprecating manner and gestured to her porcelain, makeup-free complexion, $500 vintage Betsey Johnson peasant top, and Antik Batik Foster Fringe Pouch. "One day, I'm going to have you come over to my house and go through all my clothes with your expert little eye . . ."

As Lark continued her condescension masterclass, Alison entertained thoughts of going over to the older girl's house. The thoughts ended with Lark's house in flames.

"So anyway," said Lark briskly, "is T with you? Is he around? It's imperative I see him."

Alison was suspicious. "Why?" *Not that Lark was any kind of threat, but still . . .*

Lark turned deadly earnest. "*Highlights* censored my test-question exposé!"

Alison blinked a few times. She understood the meanings of all these words. She just wasn't sure how they existed in the same sentence.

Lark broke it down for her. "*Highlights*. The school paper?"

"Right." Alison nodded. *There's a school paper?*

"I dug up hard evidence linking a prominent staff member to one of those sites that sells test questions. And now those cowards at the paper won't run it." Lark brandished her BlackBerry Curve. "So I'm organizing an emergency meeting. There's going to be an explanation from the principal or there's going to be a coup. Either way, we're having our voices heard by any means necessary!"

Changing her strident tone, Lark smiled sweetly and said, "Ooh, I love the way your eyelashes curl. One day, I gotta find out all about how that *girlie* stuff works." Then she made her way to the emergency meeting, leaving Alison feeling approximately eight years old.

No wonder he thinks I'm immature, she thought bitterly.

David and Kellyn walked toward the Hottiemobile, snapping at each other like angry rottweilers. David held the passenger door open for Kellyn with exaggerated politeness.

"After you, Freckles," said David, referring to her milky pallor.

"No, after *you*, Tiny," said Kellyn, probably not referring to his diminutive stature.

Dorinda, who *was* skilled at assuming accents and personalities, attempted to construct a sentence that revealed to David how much she liked him without actually coming right out and saying it.

"Hey, David, I've got other ideas for voices and identities; maybe we could . . ." Before she managed to finish the sentence, Alison pushed past her and jumped into the Hottiemobile. "Let's go," she instructed Designated Dean. "Let's be gone. I'm *craving* the Koo Koo Roo right now!"

"Maybe we could nothing." Dorinda sighed, climbing into

the backseat. Squeezing in next to Kellyn, she asked, "Why are you so mean to him?"

"If I'm forced to hang out with him, that's the price he has to pay."

"But you might hurt his feelings."

"He's lucky that's all I hurt" was Kellyn's reply.

At that exact moment, David was about to climb into the back of the Mercedes. That was when Kellyn—*maybe on purpose, maybe not*—yanked the door shut, closing it on his index finger. David's scream of pain reverberated inside the car and was audible all the way to the back of Nordstrom, where the trembling PBG lingered.

FOUR

Hurt

Just as he had a few months earlier, T stood in the reception area of Midway Hospital and assured a distraught Alison that David would be okay. On the previous occasion, David had bounced off the hood of T's car and wound up with a bruised coccyx.

"And he was right back on his feet," T reminded Alison, their earlier fight forgotten. "Kid's unbreakable."

"Unbearable, you mean," said Kellyn, drawing disbelieving stares from Alison.

Dorinda paced the floor, hugging herself and whispering, "Oh My God. Oh My God. I never got to tell him how much I like him."

An attending nurse approached the group. "You came with David Eels?"

"Oh My God," wailed Dorinda, struck by the fear that the only boy she ever liked might just have expired.

"He's going to be fine," said the nurse. "He just had a shock. We bandaged him up and gave him something for the pain. You can take him home in a few minutes."

Alison, Dorinda, and T gasped with relief. Alison felt tears coming into her eyes.

T hugged both girls. "It's okay," he said consolingly. "David's fine."

Kellyn stood apart from the tearful group. Part of her probably knew this was not the appropriate moment to display her contempt for their open emotion. But that part was not in control.

"Boo hoo. *Whatev.* He's *fine.* Give him a day to rest his paw, then he'll be back to his favorite pastime."

Alison broke away from T and Dorinda. She shoved her hands in her pockets, not wanting to set fire to any important hospital equipment.

"Shut up!" she shouted at Kellyn. "Just shut up. This is all your fault. You're the reason David's in here. And you're not even sorry. You think it's funny."

The other groups of anxious relatives and friends gathered in the reception area turned their collective attention to the possibility of a catfight.

T put a hand on Alison's shoulder, trying to calm her down. She shook it off.

Kellyn's face reddened. She swallowed hard.

Alison took a step forward. "I don't want you here when David comes out. He doesn't need you to make him feel worse. None of us need you. Just go home."

Kellyn's eyes flickered around the reception area. The spectators in reception seemed intrigued by her response. She looked like she wanted to run away.

"Just go," repeated Alison. "Everything's a joke to you, anyway. Make it a private joke."

"Fine," Kellyn managed to say. She moved toward the exit. "Come on, Dor." She gestured to Dorinda.

"I'm staying with David," said Dorinda.

Kellyn looked back. Three of them. All staring at her with intense, obvious dislike. One of her. Lines drawn. Kellyn nodded and opened the door. Without even looking back, she called out, "If it turns out Eels needs a new finger, I've got one he can have." With that, she raised her middle digit and disappeared through the hospital door.

FIVE
I Have a Dream

Alison had never considered herself a needy person. She could handle being alone. But that night, as she reclined on a sun lounger, watching candles shaped like blue orchids float on the surface of the hourglass pool in her spacious Brentwood backyard, she wished there was *someone* around. She wished there was *someone* to help her make sense of the thoughts that had been circling around her head ever since she returned home from the hospital. She wished she could talk to her mom. She wished her dad wasn't working all the time. But he was under the impression that criminal negligence on the part of British Airways was responsible for a giant frozen ball of poo dropping from the faulty waste tank of one of their planes and squishing his second wife. Alison hadn't yet found the right time to explain that she was the one responsible for the demise of his spouse. In fact, she doubted she'd *ever* find the right time, so she allowed her father, the noted attorney, to carry on with his massive lawsuit against the airline.

Just for a second, Alison even found herself wishing she hadn't flattened Carmen. Sure, her stepmother had turned out to be a monster. And a homicidal maniac. But she'd been *so easy to talk to*. In the few short, sweet weeks leading up to the execution of Carmen's master plan to set Alison up for a million-dollar jewelry heist, she'd been caring, compassionate, and completely nonjudgmental. *How desperately do I need someone like that in my life right now?* she thought. Someone who would let her unburden herself of the thoughts that had been swimming around her head. Someone who wouldn't immediately condemn her as a horrible person when she told them: *I need better friends.*

Alison shuddered and pulled a black-and-white woven cashmere throw around her shoulders. There they were again. Those thoughts. If only *everyone* hadn't let her down all on the same day. If only T hadn't walked away. If only he hadn't called her immature. If only Lark Rise hadn't made her feel like she really *was* immature. If only Kellyn hadn't undermined her in front of the PBG. If only David and Kellyn didn't hate each other. If only Dorinda wasn't such a passive follower. If only Kellyn had shown the slightest morsel of remorse after almost amputating David's finger. If only David hadn't been so openly derisive about her love for *Jen*.

But they had. They'd all done something to disappoint her. *I'm a superhero*, Alison thought. *I have superpowers. I fight evil, injustice, corruption, and wrongness. It should be a privilege for these people to go on mishes with me. But all they do is argue and complain and bitch and walk away.*

Aware that she was allowing her feelings of underappreciation to engulf her, Alison reached for the copy of *Jen* she'd brought back from the big box. Her mood immediately lightened. She turned to the editor's letter and found herself gazing fondly at the heart-shaped face of Pixie Furmanovsky. What did *Jen's* fifteen-year-old boss have to say to loyal reader Alison Cole of Brentwood? "I love you and appreciate you." Alison gasped at the first line of Pixie's monthly address to the *Jen* audience: "Getting the chance to run what was always, always my favorite magazine has been amazing and incredible." Pixie's letter continued, "But the best part of the job *by far* is getting to know all of you. The letters and emails I get every day are awesome and inspiring. Every time I get to meet any of you, I'm blown away by how cool and smart you are. I'm incredibly honored that you let me be part of your lives, and I know that you're going to make this world a better place. My favorite part of every month is when I get to sit down and write this letter to you. It's my chance to say thank you for letting me be part of the *Jen* family. I want you to know I take your faith in me seriously. I won't ever let you down."

Alison stared at the picture of Pixie in amazement. How could some billionaire's daughter know the exact right thing to say to her when her supposed best friends couldn't? That thought bubbled up in her head again. *I need better friends.* Which is why, five minutes later, Alison positioned her Panasonic Mini-DV camcorder on a table by the poll, returned to the sun-lounger and began to explain why she was America's No.1 *Jen* Girl. . . .

SIX
When Badfinger Met Salmonella

David pulled off the bandage and stared at his finger. The nail was black with hints of yellow. The pain medication had worn off, and it had begun throbbing. Fascinated, he reached for his phone, took a picture of his wound, and sent it off to his friend Toenail, who had undergone a similar trauma. Toenail's hideous green hangnail had eventually dropped off, but the name had stuck. David had never had a nickname before. *I like Badfinger*, he thought. Or *Black Hand. Black Hand Eels. The B.H.E. But what if someone gives me a name I don't like. Why can't I give myself a nickname?* The feedback-drenched music blasting in David's room was so loud and his internal debate about whether or not he had the right to give himself a nickname was so engrossing that it took him a second to register that Kellyn was standing by his bedroom door.

He sat on the edge of his bed and folded his arms, unconsciously adopting a defensive position. Kellyn didn't say anything at first. She looked around David's room, her brow furrowing at the proliferation of action figures and posters covering the walls. *What was Tokyo Gore Police? Who were The Mighty Boosh? And what was that noise?*

"What are you listening to? It sounds like bees. Is it bees?"

"It's the Jesus and Mary Chain," said David, not meeting her eyes. "They're from the '80s."

"I don't know how you can listen to that."

"Me neither. Maybe you should slam a car door *on my ear*."

Kellyn's shoulders slumped. She looked pale and unhappy. Which was pretty much how she always looked. But this was different. Usually, Kellyn's face reflected her contempt for everybody and everything she encountered. Now she looked sad and a little bit lost. To David's surprise, she walked across the room and stood by his bed. She paused for a second, as if she were waiting for permission. Then she went to sit next to him. Halfway down, she realized his comforter might be sheltering alien substances, so she picked up a magazine to use as a cushion. It wasn't until she actually sat down that she was struck by the thought that the magazine was even more likely to contain alien substances.

David said nothing. Kellyn had made the move. It was up to her to do the talking. Speaking in a small voice, she said, "I love Alison, you know. It's amazingly generous of her to stay friends with me after everything I've said and done. But I used to be jealous of her because she was so popular and pretty, and now she's a *superhero*. And I see the way you and T look at her. How amazing you think she is. And I do, too. But at the same time, all I can think is no one will ever look at me like that. The only way I can compete with her is to be meaner than she is. That's my only talent."

"It's a big talent," observed David.

"Huge," agreed Kellyn. "If I had an evil alias, I'd be Salmonella. I poison everything." David looked impressed and thought, *She gave herself a nickname, why can't I?*

Kellyn went on, "But I have to consciously try to not be mean to her because I'm already so guilty about what I did. So I've got all this *stuff* building up inside me, and it's got to go somewhere. So I give it to you. Both barrels."

David looked surprised. "See, I thought we were having fun. I thought that was our *thing*. The bickering sidekicks."

"I know," said Kellyn, staring intently at him. "No matter how vicious I get, you throw it straight back in my face. And that just makes me feel worse. It's like, if I can't even hurt some dork, what's the point of me?"

David's face grew cold. "Okay. Thanks for the heartfelt apology. Close the door on your way out."

The screeching Jesus and Mary Chain track ended. The subsequent silence felt much louder.

Kellyn inched closer to David, her eyes moistening. "I'm hard to like, I know I am. But I had a bunch of people who made an effort to include me in their lives, and I went out of my way to alienate them all. And I hurt you and I'm sorry."

David had seen Kellyn apologize to Alison in the past. He

knew she was capable of sincerity. But he had never seen her this vulnerable.

"I'm so mean," she said in a whisper. "I'm *so* mean."

"You're not *that* mean," said David. Then he found himself laughing. "You nearly leave me fingerless, and I'm trying to make *you* feel better."

Kellyn almost managed a smile. She reached toward his wounded hand. David started to draw back.

"It's okay," she murmured. "Let me."

Kellyn curled her fingers around his palm and raised it to her face. She stared at the blackened fingernail.

"What do you think of Badfinger as a nickname? Kinda hood, right?" David asked.

Kellyn blinked back tears as she stared at his finger. *My fault*, she thought. *All my fault.* She blew gently on David's finger as if it would blow away all the pain she felt and all the hurt she'd caused. David shivered. Then Kellyn touched his fingertip to her lips.

He stared at her. She looked up at him, reached out, put her arms around his neck, brought his face close to hers, and then they kissed.

Their eyes were closed. Another Jesus and Mary Chain song, even louder and buzzier than the last one, blasted out of the speakers. Neither of them heard the two knocks on the door. Neither of them were aware that Dorinda had walked into the room, carrying a bottle of black nail polish, which she'd brought to paint David's nonbruised nails so he wouldn't have to be reminded of the accident. Neither of them heard her gasp and run out of the bedroom.

SEVEN

Are You There, Jen? It's Me, Hottie

The beautiful blonde lolled on the sun lounger. She took a sip of her Coke and grapefruit cocktail. Then she reached for a copy of *Pink Sugar*, the widely read teen magazine, and began skimming its pages.

"Boring." She sighed, tossing it aside.

Then she picked up another magazine. The beautiful blonde got maybe two pages into the second one before discarding it with a yawn. The same fate happened to two, three, four more magazines. Suddenly, there was quite a pile. Finally, the beautiful blonde opened the latest edition of *Jen*.

"Awesome." She smiled. And then she addressed the camera. "*Jen*'s always been the best. It treats me like I'm special. It rocks my world. And it lets me know what's hot . . ." And then the beautiful blonde pointed her finger at the pile of discarded magazines. A burst of flame shot out from her finger and reduced the rival magazines to a mound of smoking ashes. The beautiful blonde smiled at the camera. "And what's not," she said.

The Jen.com staffer charged with sifting through the *Jen* Girl competition entries cc'd the clip to everyone at the magazine. Soon the staff was buzzing about the beautiful blonde. Who was she? How did she do that?

"Duh," yawned an unimpressed copy editor. "She's an LA chick. She's got industry connections up the wazooty. It's so obvious she got some CGI nerd to magic her up a special effect. Wasn't even a particularly good one. You look closely, and you can see it's fake."

That dissenting voice aside, *Jen* was collectively wowed by the clip of the beautiful blonde. Which is how Alison shot to the top of the list of candidates vying to become America's No. 1 *Jen* Girl.

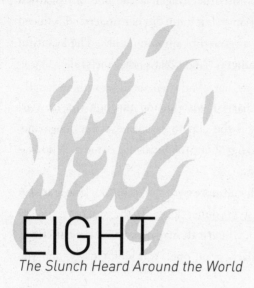

EIGHT
The Slunch Heard Around the World

Kellyn had no idea Dorinda was about to hit her. She thought her friend was reaching out to push a stray lock of brown hair behind her ear or rub a smudge of dirt off her face. Dorinda had no idea she was about to hit Kellyn. But the years of being the faithful follower, of being ignored and underestimated and taken for granted, *of pretending to be French* . . . and now having the first boy she ever really liked cruelly snatched away from under her nose . . . *something snapped.*

On the way to school, Dorinda had convinced herself she hadn't seen what she thought she'd seen the night before. *They weren't kissing. They couldn't have been kissing. Kellyn wouldn't do that to me. She* knows *how much I like him. She was apologizing for being mean. That's all. She's a warm person. Deep down. I overreacted.*

I shouldn't have run away. And even if they were *kissing, they probably started fighting three seconds later. But they* weren't *kissing.*

And then she'd seen the limo service provided by Kellyn's rarely present mother pull up outside the school. And then she'd seen Kellyn and *David* get out. And then she'd seen them laughing *and* play *fighting* as they made their way up the steps. And then Kellyn had waved at her and gestured at her to wait. And then she'd waited for her best friend and the guy she'd never got around to telling how much she liked. And then there was some incredible geek emergency that required David to scurry off and confer with his bizarre friends. And after Kellyn watched him go, *with a big happy smile on her face*, she'd taken Dorinda's arm.

"Here's the plan," she'd said. "Slow but gradual transformation. So he doesn't see it coming. Get him a decent haircut. Then human clothes. I'll take him shopping. You can come, too . . ."

And then Dorinda had pulled her arm away from Kellyn and stared at her best friend. Dorinda had never hit anyone before, so the thing that flew at Kellyn's face was a mixture of curled hand and extended thumb. It wasn't quite a slap, but neither was it a punch. It was a *slunch*. The impact of the slunch caused Kellyn's mouth to fall open in total surprise. It also caused camera phones around the steps of the school to start clicking. In a matter of minutes, viral videos of the slunch would flood cyberspace.

Alison shoved her way through the camera-toting hordes. She flew up the steps, grabbed Kellyn and Dorinda by the wrists, and dragged them into school.

"*Ow!*" screamed Kellyn.

"*Ow!*" echoed Dorinda.

Alison's hands were *hot*. She didn't care. She pulled the two struggling, squealing foes through the hallway and shoved them into the girls' room, the thought *I need better friends* pinballing inside her head the whole way.

"Get. Out. Now," snarled Alison to the freshmen fixing their faces in the bathroom. They took one look at Alison's thunderous expression and fled.

Alison stared at her two best friends in disbelief. "*Well?*" she demanded.

"She hit me!" exclaimed Kellyn. She went over to the mirror, saw the reddening thumbprint under her eye, and gasped.

Alison put her hands on her hips and looked at Dorinda. "*Well?*"

Dorinda said nothing for a moment. Then she spoke. "She kissed David."

Alison looked baffled. "David who?"

"David *Eels!*" exclaimed Dorinda.

Alison was still baffled. "The David Eels that we know?"

"She knew I liked him, and she kissed him."

Kellyn turned from the mirror and looked at Dorinda, aghast. "I didn't know you liked him."

Alison stared at her two friends. "Wait a minute, one of you likes him, and one of you *kissed* him?"

Dorinda shook her head at Kellyn. "How could you not know I liked him?"

"You never said anything."

Dorinda gave a harsh mirthless laugh. "I talked about it all the time. You just never listened. Because you never listen to me. *Ever.*"

Kellyn had never seen Dorinda like this. "That's totally not true."

"Name three things you like about me," said Dorinda, snapping her fingers three times for emphasis. "Don't think about it. Just tell me off the top of your head."

Kellyn was completely rattled. "I don't have to tell you."

Dorinda laughed bitterly. "Three things. And you can't even do that."

Kellyn held up a finger. "You're a good friend." A second finger. "You're loyal." Third finger. "I can tell you anything."

"Three things *about* me," yelled Dorinda. "Not three things about how I relate to you. About what a faithful servant I am. See, you don't *listen!*"

The bathroom door began to open. Alison pointed her finger. A jet of flame engulfed the door handle, causing the girl holding the other side to scream in pain.

Alison turned back to Kellyn and Dorinda, both red-faced, both breathing hard. "This is crazy. You've been friends forever. Don't fall out over a boy. *Especially* David Eels."

"What's wrong with David Eels?" demanded both Kellyn and Dorinda.

"Nothing." Alison sighed. "I love David. I was friends with him before either of you even knew he existed."

"Of course, of course" Kellyn nodded bitterly. "He's Alison's adoring sidekick. That's his anointed role. We're not allowed to touch him. We're not good enough."

Alison looked exasperated. *How is this being turned on me? I'm not the bad guy here! I'm the good guy. Treasure Spinney's stand-in actually believed I was an angel!*

Dorinda stabbed a finger at Kellyn, who reared back like she was about be slunched a second time. "You took the only boy I ever liked. You knew I liked him, and you went ahead and did it anyway. You are *merde* to me," she said, reverting briefly to her faux-French roots. Dorinda went to make a big dramatic exit from the bathroom but forgot the door handle was still hot and mewled in pain.

"Go after her," Alison begged Kellyn. Alison might have thought she needed better friends, but that didn't mean she wanted to see her old ones at each other's throats.

"Why?" Kellyn shrugged. "To get hit again? You saw her face. She hates me. Maybe we outgrew each other. It happens."

"But we're a *team*," implored Alison. "We're the Department of Hotness."

"So we should put aside our differences so that Alison has her group of obedient underlings around her? So that you get what you want? Like always."

"Oh, shut up, Kellyn, when do I ever get what I want?" Alison's iPhone vibrated. She grabbed it, glared at Kellyn, and snapped, "Yes?" Then she listened intently as she was informed she'd just become America's No. 1 *Jen* Girl. Alison clicked the phone off. She let a big warm wave of happiness burst over her. Then she turned to Kellyn, eager to share the unbelievable news. "You'll never believe what happened . . ." she gasped. But the bathroom was empty.

NINE
What Not to Wear

Cutesy Woo sat behind the reception desk at *Jen*. Her silky black hair cascaded over her shoulders. Her eyes were a transfixing shade of turquoise. Her nose was tiny. Her teeth were little shining pearls. She filled the air with the heady scent of jasmine. Her smile was serene, and her laughter was like the tinkling of tiny bells.

If that's the receptionist, what do the staff look like? wondered Alison as she perched on the edge of the clear-plastic Phillipe Stark chair in the reception area and acted like she didn't know she was on display.

It had probably been a little impulsive to go running out of school and back to Brentwood before the lunch bell, but after the news broke that Alison had been chosen as America's No. 1 *Jen* Girl, a *second* call from her favorite magazine emphasized how excited they were to meet her and how they couldn't *wait* for her to appear in the office. Alison figured she was justified in taking the rest of the day off, being as she was legitimately frazzled by the Kellyn/Dorinda slunch (*Over David Eels? Really?*) Plus, she *really* needed time to herself so she could work out exactly what she was going to wear on this, *the* most momentous day of her young but already-momentous life.

Just after two thirty that afternoon, Alison sat in the back of the Hottiemobile as Designated Dean drove her into the heart of Century City. The business center on the West Side of LA played home to movie studios, record labels, law offices, and multimedia corporations. But, as far as Alison was concerned, none of these other places even existed. She barely even registered the looks of horror Designated Dean was attracting as he tossed his Burger King wrapper out of the Mercedes window. Her mind was occupied with one thing and one thing only. The big glass building that housed her favorite magazine. The big glass building she was about to enter.

Minutes later, she walked out of the elevator on the twenty-third floor and entered the Temple of *Jen*. Alison gasped when she saw the blowups of previous bestselling covers lining the walls. She gasped again when the covers made eye contact with her and broke into giant smiles and silent laughter. The walls of the *Jen* office were, on closer inspection, filled with plasma screens showing live-action footage of *Jen* cover shoots. Wherever you looked, there was a teen star stuck in a video loop. Alison gasped some more when she saw that the entire reception desk was bedazzled and finally she gasped when she saw the receptionist.

Cutesy Woo's lineless brow furrowed ever so slightly when her amazing eyes took in the entirety of Alison.

"Yes?" she said in a teeny voice.

"I'm Alison Cole?" Alison said, her head swimming in the scent of jasmine. "America's No. 1 *Jen* Girl?"

Cutesy Woo gazed at Alison for what seemed like a perfumed eternity. Then she raised a graceful, bangle-laden arm and pointed Alison to the clear plastic seats. "Someone will see you soon," she barely said. Then she whispered into her earpiece, and, seconds later, the staff of *Jen* began pouring out of their workspaces and making *urgent and entirely necessary* trips to the bedazzled reception desk. A gap-toothed Somalian girl pushed a rack of clothes up to the desk, shot a quick glance at Alison, stifled a snort of laughter, and then pushed the rack back to the fashion department. The rotund beauty editor made her way toward the desk, glanced subtly around, covered her mouth when she saw Alison, then hurried back to her lair. The wheelchair-bound photographer rolled up, bit her lip when she caught sight of Alison, and sped off in fits of giggles. After a few more of these drive-bys, Alison got it. The *Jen* staff weren't checking out the new girl. They were checking out the new girl's hilarious fashion faux pas. At first, she tingled with annoyance. Who did these ordinary, average, unexceptional nobodies think they were to laugh at her? None of them looked like they belonged in the hallowed hallways of a style-and-beauty bible the caliber of *Jen*. Yet, Alison observed, none of them carried themselves with anything less than total confidence. None of them looked the least bit awkward. If anything, it was the luminous Cutesy Woo who seemed somewhat intimidated and eager to please. Every time a new member of the *Jen* staff walked, wheeled, or hobbled their way up to Cutesy's desk, she blinked, blushed, and bit her lip like she was eager for their approval. And every one of them ignored her. It was as if the standard of beauty had been reversed inside the walls of *Jen*. Perfection was frowned upon. Flaws were *fabulous*.

A shovel-chinned entertainment editor made the final journey to the reception desk. She was wearing a vintage minidress made from linked circles of mirrored metal. Alison caught fragmented glimpses of herself in the girl's shimmering garment. She had always wanted to be one of *Jen*'s Sidewalk Supermodels. But Alison had never really blazed her own trail and displayed her unique sense of style. Sure, she'd put together the Hottie costume. But there was *another* look, a classic look, that she *loved* and always had a hunch was about to explode in the streets and clubs and on catwalks across the world. Alison had always been amazed when flicking through fashion magazines that this particular look hadn't undergone a massive revival. Clearly, it was going to take the right person to bring it back. *And I'm the right person*, Alison had thought. And it had seemed perfect in the privacy of her Brentwood bedroom. But, reflected in the girl's mirrored dress, Alison saw things somewhat differently.

She saw her tomato red blazer and skirt. The metal wings pinned to her lapel. The red-and-white polka-dot scarf knotted around her neck. The scarlet hat on her head. *Maybe I'm not the right person to bring back the 1960s air stewardess look*, she concluded sadly.

And suddenly, she was flooded with insecurity and trepidation. Suddenly, she wanted to flee the twenty-third floor before the cleaning staff showed up and began pelting her with wet sponges and laughing in her face. That was the moment Cutesy Woo said, "Pixie is ready for you."

TEN
Pixie

Alison followed the receptionist to a white office door with the words PIXIE'S PALACE scrolled in pink glitter.

"*Ta-dah!*" exclaimed Cutesy Woo, throwing the door open.

"*Ta-dah!*" didn't do justice to the huge office. Alison struggled to take in the candy-striped wallpaper, the crystal chandelier, the big inviting cushions scattered across the ankle-high fluffy white shag carpet, the glitter-encrusted desk, and *the throne* by the window. This wasn't a workplace so much as an invitation to a permanent sleepover. The walls of the office celebrated Pixie Furmanovsky's triumphant resurrection of *Jen*. The left side was filled with framed front covers, each one a bigger seller than the last. The far wall had a few pictures of Pixie with smiling celebrities at her side. These pictures all contained personalized messages.

Alison peered closely at a photograph of Pixie standing next to a rising TV actress. "Thank you for keeping me off the What's Not List," the message read. The other celebrity photos contained similar expressions of gratitude. Alison was still staring at the opulence of the office when she felt a sharp tug at her wrist. She looked down. A girl was gazing up at Alison from the comfort of a cushion. She had a heart-shaped face, a head of unruly brown curls, and huge saucer-shaped eyes. She wore a red-and-white-striped rugby top and a tiny denim skirt. She was fifteen and barely five feet tall. She was the editor of the country's best-loved teen magazine.

"Oh my *gosh*," she gasped. "America's No. 1 *Jen* Girl! How awesome is that?" Pixie tightened her grip on Alison's wrist and pulled her toward the cushions. "Scrunch down, and we'll get to know each other," she ordered.

Alison let herself sink into an all-enveloping marshmallow of a cushion. Pixie held out her arms for a hug. Alison hesitated for a second and then submitted to the embrace.

"I'm *so* glad you're here," said Pixie softly. "We're going to have so much fun."

The warm, welcoming quality so evident in Pixie's monthly editor's letter was magnified a million times in person. She might be a tycoon's daughter, but Pixie had the gift of making everyone she encountered feel like the most important person in the world. With her huge eyes brimming with sincerity, she told Alison why she had selected her as America's No. 1 *Jen* Girl. ("There was something about you. You're this pretty, perfect LA blonde, but you're *so* not. There's so much more going on with you. Like that outfit. Who would wear something like that if they weren't completely bizarre? And I love that.") She talked about her philosophy of *Jen*. ("There's no difference to me between the editor and the reader. We're all part of the same family. We're all going through the same stuff. I want everyone who reads *Jen* to know that I'm just like them. I'm real just like them. I struggle with the same issues they do. And so does everyone on staff. You've seen the girls who work here. They'd be amazing at any other magazine. But no other magazine would hire them. They're all desperate for their staff to look beyond fabulous. They only want to hire blondes and Brazilians who need guidebooks to unscrew their water bottles. So I get my pick of the best.") She talked about being a fifteen-year-old editor. ("I know what all those old ladies who run the other magazines think. That I'm a joke. That I asked my daddy to buy *Jen* for me like it's a Chanel clutch bag I'm desperate to have and then throw away after the first time I wear it out. I love that they think that. It's awesome to be underestimated.") And she talked about her father. ("My daddy's a serious businessman. He wouldn't have bought the magazine if he thought I was going to get bored with it. He knows he did the right thing investing in me. I get emails from him all the time telling me what a good job I'm doing.")

Finally, Pixie paused for breath. She glanced at the Concord Crystale around her wrist. Alison shot a discreet peek at her own watch. Ninety minutes had elapsed since she had sat down next to Pixie. It barely seemed like five.

"Boring bit over," announced Pixie. "On to the important stuff. *Guys.* So have you got, like, a hundred and fifty boyfriends?"

Alison winced. "I'm not sure I even have one."

Pixie made a buzzing sound. "Lie detector disagrees."

"It's complicated," said Alison. But even as she was sending out a signal that she wanted the subject changed, Alison found herself thinking, *She's just like me. She's going through the same stuff. Why shouldn't I confide in her?* Pushing herself to an upright position, Alison began. "There is someone. He's older."

"Ooh," squeaked Pixie. "Clooney older? Pitt older?"

"He's a junior," said Alison.

Pixie waved a dismissive hand in the air. "Uncrushworthy!" she snapped.

Alison was about to launch into a rant about the injustice of T's perception of her as immature. But she never got the chance.

"*Project!*" sang out Pixie. "We'll find you a molten hot guy— not some *junior*—and you can bring him to my sweet sixteen. It's going to be epic, thus you need an epic date. But not *too* epic. He can't outshine mine. And mine's gonna be the date to end all dates, you won't even believe it. Let me think, who can we dig up? . . ."

Inspired, Pixie jumped up and skipped to her glittery desk. Once ensconced behind her throne, she began tapping at her computer. "Him?" she mused to the computer screen. "Nah. Loser. This one? Cute but he wears those Ed Hardy T-shirts I hate to the very core of my being. This guy? Mmm. Maybe. We'll put a pin in him for now."

Alison felt a burst of panic as she watched Pixie at work. She didn't want a new boyfriend. She wanted a chastened, apologetic, respectful old boyfriend. But Pixie seemed a little bit . . . *undeniable.* Alison pushed herself out of the pillow and got to her feet.

She walked around the office. The framed photos on the wall weren't all celeb photo ops and *Jen* covers. There were other photographs. Preteen Pixie and a distinguished-looking older man in Rome. Pixie and the man in London. At the White House. Lots of impressive locations. Every photo featuring only Pixie and the older man.

"Is it just you and your dad, Pixie?" asked Alison.

"Since I was six," she said, still looking at her computer screen. "Just before my birthday."

Alison nodded. She felt momentarily guilty for navigating what had been a get-to-know-you meeting into such intensely personal waters. But even though they'd just met, Alison felt close to Pixie. Like she could ask her anything. "Ten for me. Just after New Year's."

Pixie stopped tapping at the keyboard. She looked up at Alison. Her eyes weren't so huge and earnest anymore. There was no dazzling smile lighting up the room. No *Surrender to My Charisma*. Alison was suddenly aware that behind the whole *Win! Achieve! Inspire!* side of Pixie that made her so . . . *undeniable*, there was someone else. Someone who had forced herself to grow up before she was ready but still had a part of her that ached to be a normal girl and to have a normal friend. *And I will be that normal friend*, thought Alison.

Pixie was also aware that something had changed between them. They weren't just the new *Jen* girl and the magazine prodigy. They were suddenly teetering on the brink of becoming close.

"Get your phone out, girl," Pixie exclaimed. "I need all your info."

Alison pulled out her iPhone. Pixie produced . . . it was the same shape as her iPhone. But it was smaller, thinner, encased in pink, and it glittered. Alison took a closer look at Pixie's phone. It was pink, and it glittered because it was covered in pink diamonds. *Real* pink diamonds. Pixie captured Alison's slack-jawed expression with a click of her phone. Then she pressed a button on the keyboard. Suddenly, Alison's slack-jawed impression was a 3-D holographic image floating above the phone.

"That was mean." Pixie laughed. "Give me a better pose. Give me America's No. 1 *Jen* Girl."

Alison attempted to strike a model-esque pose. Pixie clicked her pink-diamond phone, and the image of Alison with her mouth hanging open was replaced with a more-acceptable picture.

Alison pointed at Pixie's phone and moaned simply, "Want."

"Can't have. Not yet, anyway. This is the next-next-next-*next* generation model. It's the only one there is. The guys at my daddy's nerd factory even customized it for me. Look." Pixie held the phone up to Alison's face. The screen showed the word *pixiePhone*. "But they're always beavering away on something new. They never see the sun. They're like vampires. Unbelievably unsexy vampires. Once they're done with the next-next-next-next-next model, you can have this one." Pixie touched another key. A 3-D hologram of her address book hung in the air. "Key in all your deets," she said.

But just as Alison was about to reach for the pink-diamond phone of the future, Pixie yelped, "I'm so rude. I never asked you if you wanted something to drink. Or eat. You must, right? We've been talking for *days*!"

Alison didn't have a chance to reply before Pixie touched another key. The sound of a bell rang loudly from the phone's speakers. Pixie winked at Alison and whispered, "Wait." She looked at her door. Alison followed her gaze. A knock on the door.

"Come," said Pixie.

The door opened. A waiter walked in, pencil and notebook at the ready.

"We'll have two bottles of Vitaminwater, the apple-blue-berry and the lemon-lime. And bring us a nice selection of Cold Stone Creamery sorbets: lemon, raspberry, watermelon, and tangerine."

The waiter took down Pixie's order. Alison watched him work. He looked to be in his early thirties. His shoes were Barneys leather loafers. He wore a Breitling watch around his wrist. His hair was expensively styled.

Pixie leaned over and whispered in Alison's ear. "He's Avril Lavigne's publicist. He promised he'd do whatever it took for us to put his client back on the What's Hot List. Avril's a doll, and she'll totally be back in the magazine, but he offered, so why not? It's fun, right?"

Alison was about to laugh. Then she saw the look in the man's eyes. He didn't look like he was having fun. The man saw her looking and backed quickly out of the office. Alison stared at Pixie, jaw slack one last time.

"I hope I never make the Not list," she said.

Pixie put an arm around her new friend's waist. "The list is fluff. Nobody really takes it seriously. But don't worry, you're under my wing. Nothing bad's going to happen to you while we're friends. And we *are* friends, aren't we, Allywally?"

We're at the pet-name stage already? worried Alison. But then she thought, *I've been around backstabbers and grudge-holders too long. I've forgotten that some people are actually nice. And she's so nice.* "We sure are, Pixie Stix," enthused Alison.

Pixie beamed with pleasure at being re-petted. "So what are your exciting plans for tonight?" she asked.

Alison was taken by surprise. Close as she'd immediately become to Pixie, she still wasn't about to admit she usually spent her nights battling evil with a bunch of ungrateful misfits. "Well . . ." she began.

"Wrong answer!" yelled Pixie.

"What's the right answer?"

Pixie flashed a billion-dollar grin. "It involves a swimsuit . . ."

ELEVEN

Ballbuster

$\mathscr{A}$lison sighed with contentment. It was a combination of the Malibu night sky, the feel of the warm sand under her feet, and the light wind as it played in her hair.

"Don't get too used to this," warned a voice.

Alison looked around. Standing next to her, she saw Amandine, the rotund fashion editor, a half-eaten hot dog in her hand. She was one of the many *Jen* staffers who had expressed their nonverbal opinion of Alison's choice of get-to-know-you attire.

"Don't count on invitations to Pixie's beach house becoming a regular event." Before Alison could react, Amandine broke into a huge sunny grin. "Sometimes you're gonna be sleeping over at the penthouse she has at the Peninsula. Sometimes we spend weekends at the Bellagio in Vegas, baby. If her dad's private jet is free, we fly to Paris . . ."

The gap-toothed Somalian girl, whose name was Waris, joined them. "Sometimes we get to see sneak previews of movies before anyone—the director, the stars, the studio people—sees them."

Elspeth, the wheelchair-bound photographer, navigated her way through the sand. "And sometimes she closes down Disneyland just so we don't have to wait in line."

Alison looked at the wide smiling faces of her new colleagues. She had felt a brief burst of concern when Pixie had invited her to an impromptu midweek party at her beach house. She had felt even more concern when she found herself bundled into the back of a stretch limo with the staffers, who had checked her out earlier and found her wanting. But, by the time the limo pulled away from the magazine's Century City nerve center and headed toward the Pacific Coast Highway, whatever suspicion had initially existed about the new *Jen* girl on the block had become a distant memory. The *Jen* staffers couldn't have been sweeter or funnier. Pixie's gorgeous, glass-walled Malibu beach house couldn't have been more luxurious, and the stretch of private beach that lay a stone's throw away from the back porch couldn't have been more inviting. For the first time in a long time, Alison wasn't spending her after-school hours on the trail of increasingly unthreatening evildoers, she wasn't enduring the barbs of her friends, she wasn't wondering what was going on in her boyfriend's head. Instead, she was swimming, she was barbecuing, she was relaxing, and she was hanging out with a crew of unexpectedly cool girls who seemed to have accepted her without a hidden agenda.

"Don't ruin my image," called out Pixie. "I'm a tough boss. I'm tyrannical!" All the *Jen* girls turned around to see their editor looking adorable as she came padding out of the ocean.

The staff watched her as she tried to shake the strands of seaweed that had snagged themselves around her ankle. They were all thinking the same thing. *She's so tiny and so cute. Yet she runs this multimillion-dollar magazine.* Alison caught the look of awe on the faces of her new workmates. And found herself sharing in the pride they had for where they worked and who they worked for. It was a warm moment. It ended seconds later when a volleyball slammed into the fashion editor, knocking her hot dog to the ground.

The sound of hands clapping echoed across the beach. "Ball!" yelled a chorus of raucous voices. The *Jen* staff turned to see a group of bare-chested guys and bikini-clad girls, all in their late teens, all of whom were behaving like their lives were an eternal spring break.

"Ball!" they howled. Waris kicked the ball back to them.

"Guys, this is a private beach," Pixie called over to the interlopers. "I'm okay with you hanging out for a while but be cool, okay?"

Shouts of "Yes, ma'am!" greeted Pixie's request. She walked across the sand and rejoined her staff.

"They're kids." She shrugged. "We've all done worse."

The group nodded. Then the volleyball hit the wheelchair-bound Elspeth on the side of the head. Amid hoots of laughter, one of the beach crashers ambled up to the shocked *Jen* girls. He was all sinew and six-pack, with a broad insolent smirk on his face that only increased in size as he got a clear view of his victims. A heavyset girl. A wheelchair resident. A gap-toothed Somalian. A teeny-tiny girl with seaweed wrapped around her ankle. Amusement danced in his eyes as he appraised and dismissed the *Jen* girls. Finally, he addressed Alison, the only member of the group who seemed to him as if she remotely belonged in such inviting surroundings.

"Sorry about that, sparklehorse," he drawled. "I'll try and exercise better ball control." He looked down at the dazed Elspeth. "You okay there, little guy? Nothing broken? I mean, apart from the obvious." Alison felt her fingers start to burn. She looked at the faces of the *Jen* staff. All the confidence that Pixie had instilled in them had vanished. They weren't walking the halls of *Jen* now. They were out in the real world, where cocky, uncaring guys like this treated them like the poo under his shoes.

"It takes the cops six seconds to get here," warned Pixie.

"Don't call the po-po. We'll be good. I promise." The guy grinned as he scooped up the ball and swaggered back to his friends, who were doubled over with laughter.

"Let's go inside," said Pixie.

"It's getting cold," The fashion editor nodded.

And then, just loud enough to hear, one of the beach crashers chuckled, saying, "A hundred dollars if you knock the gimp right off her chair this time."

Alison didn't even pause to consider her actions. She spun around. The volleyball was flying toward the *Jen* girls. She broke into a run, launched herself into the air, and slammed a burning hand into the ball. Suddenly, it was a molten orb of fiery leather, and it was flying straight toward the huddle of intruders. Their laughter abruptly stopped. They broke into a run and narrowly avoided the volleyball as it landed in the pile of their discarded clothes and shoes. Alison approached them, slightly breathless, her hands in fists by her side.

The taunting smile had entirely left the guy with the sinews and the six-pack. She stared them down for a moment. Then she snarled, "I'll try and exercise better ball control."

The guys in the group looked at each other, all hoping one of them was about to show this suddenly scary blonde girl she'd messed with the wrong crew. It quickly became evident that none of them were going to do it. Alison didn't even allow herself the satisfaction of watching them flee in terror. As she made the journey back to the *Jen* girls, she could hear the intruders running from the beach. Even before she returned to Pixie and the others, she heard the screams. And they weren't screams of terror.

"Whoooo!" shrieked Waris, crushing Alison in a hug. "I don't know what you did, but you took care of business, you little badass, you!"

The other girls joined in the congratulatory huddle. Only Pixie stood apart from the group of gushing, grateful staffers.

Elspeth grinned up at the editor. "Oh My God, Pixie. Alison is *amazing.* She totally saved us!"

Pixie's face was momentarily blank. "Yes," she said, a little coolly. "Because it's not like I could have done anything. It's only my house and my beach."

Alison glanced over at Pixie, surprised by her tone. Then Pixie's eyes grew huge, and her smile lit up the night. "I was *so* right making you America's No. 1 *Jen* Girl!" Then she hugged Alison tightly.

TWELVE

War

"*Uh-oh*," *said Alison* as she looked through her emails the following morning and saw the invitation. "Kellyn Levy added you as a friend on Facebook," said the subject matter.

Kellyn had made it clear she was not a Facebook fan. "If I want to know what you're doing right this moment, I'll ask you. And if you really think I'm interested in what you're doing, then you obviously don't know me. And if you don't know me, why would I want to be pretend friends with you?" was Kellyn's reasoning.

Even as Alison followed the link to confirm the friend request, she knew what she'd find. *Except this was worse. Far far worse.* Alison stared at the picture. Kellyn in a T-shirt that said, It's Not My Fault God Made You Ugly, Fat, and Stupid. Alison vividly recalled having the shirt made for Kellyn's thirteenth birthday. *As a joke*! An acknowledgment of Kellyn's misanthropic tendencies. Which even Kellyn recognized as funny. The day the photo had been taken was the only time she had ever worn it. *But only a really, really good friend would know that.*

With a heavy heart, Alison scrolled down the fake Facebook page. The minifeed said, "Kellyn thinks Alison Cole is desperate for the approval of others." The entries beneath listed Kellyn's opinions about other BHHS students and staff members. They were equally harsh. Under "Personal Info," the entry read, "Stepping over anyone who gets in my way and laughing while I cheat and lie my way to the top. Ha ha!"

Alison thought back to her blissful night at Pixie's beach house. She'd known her new *Jen* friends for what didn't really amount to much more than a matter of minutes. But she had no doubt that if she was in desperate need, any one of them would willingly give her a bone-marrow transplant. Not only was that something she could not say about her old set of friends, but on this morning's evidence, she didn't even think she could stop Dorinda from stealing Kellyn's kidney and selling it on eBay.

Alison walked out of her bedroom. She hurried down the caramel-carpeted staircase, passing a series of framed photographs that charted her evolution from cherubic toddler to dazzling young woman. Alison slowed down as she reached the bottom of the steps. Dorinda was standing in the middle of the hallway. She held out two T-shirts. In her left hand, she was holding a shirt that had the message TEAM DORINDA on it. In the other, a shirt that read, TEAM KELLEN.

Alison stopped before she reached the last step. "That one's misspelled," she said.

"THEN DON'T WEAR IT!" Dorinda bawled. "Wear the right one!" She threw the TEAM DORINDA T-shirt at Alison.

Alison hurled the shirt back at Dorinda. "Stop this. Take the fake Kellyn Facebook page down. Take it down *now*."

Dorinda was almost shaking with righteous indignation. "I'm justified. I'm the wronged party. Anything I do is okay. Tell *her* to stop. . . ."

Alison reached for her friend's hands. "Dor, this isn't you. . . ."

Dorinda snatched her hands away. "How do you know? You don't know me. You don't care."

Alison watched Dorinda pace the hallway. "Of *course* I care. I've been hurt before. I know what it's like. You play it over and over in your mind. You keep obsessing about what you could have done different."

"This is really helping. Thanks so much," said Dorinda sarcastically.

"It'll get better, though. But not if you do stuff like this. You're lashing out because you want revenge. But revenge makes you . . ." Alison stopped and gazed at her friend, who was still stomping around the hallway, pounding her Ann Demeulemeester lace-up sandal boots off the pristine dark gray marble flooring. Dorinda's thick shiny hair was flying. Her impressive boobage was bouncing unrestrained inside her tight TEAM DORINDA T-shirt. *Revenge had made her hot.*

Alison tried a different tack. "Here's the three things I like about you. Ready?" Dorinda stopped walking. Alison counted out on her fingers. "One: You're beautiful. I always thought that. Two: You're amazingly talented. I'm still not sure if you're a French girl pretending to be American or the other way around. Three: Honestly, I like that you like David. It shows how un-shallow you are."

Dorinda threw the T-shirt back in Alison's face. "So you're on my side."

Alison let the shirt fall to the floor. "Don't make me choose between my friends. I won't do it."

"But you *have* chosen, Miss Superhero," said Dorinda, stomp-ing her way to the front door of the Coles' mansion. "You were presented with a clear case of right versus wrong, and you have elected to stay in the middle of the road and allow wrong to flour-ish. You're as bad as *that other girl* is. One day, you will realize this, and you will come to me and admit I was right. But I won't be around to hear your apology because we are done. *Au revoir!*"

The door slammed shut behind Dorinda. Alison stood alone in the hallway. The sound of their shrill argument still echoed faintly around the house. "Uh-oh," said Alison to herself again.

Two hours later, Kellyn sat in American history surrounded by classmates who had received invitations to join the phony Facebook page Dorinda had put up under Kellyn's name. Hostile looks and angry whispers filled the classroom. Kellyn showed no sign of noticing. Dorinda, sitting on the other side of the class-room, was also on the receiving end of attention and discussion. Her revenge-fueled hotness was being appreciated by a wide selection of BHHS male students.

Suddenly, everyone stopped paying attention to the estranged pair and focused on the plight of Brie Feltz. Alison's onetime rival for the freshman presidency had just dumped the contents of her bag on the floor and was down on her knees, searching frantically through the upended items.

"I can't find my inhaler!" she cried out. "Where's my inhaler? Did someone take it?"

The teacher reacted to Brie's rising panic. "Everybody check and see if you picked up Brie's inhaler by mistake."

The students went through their bags and pockets. Brie wheezed dramatically. "That's what it sounds like when I have an attack," she explained.

Dorinda felt inside her Louis Vuitton Laundry Bag. Her fingers made contact with an unfamiliar object. She knew what it was and how it got there. Brie wheezed again. This time it wasn't a demonstration. Dorinda pulled out the inhaler and hurried over to Brie.

"You stole my inhaler," wheezed Brie accusingly. "You're not supposed to be the mean one."

Dorinda was about to declare her innocence. Then she glanced over at Kellyn and saw the fake-shocked look on her face. Dorinda slunk back to her seat, the accusing eyes of the teacher and the rest of the class trained on her. Dorinda's phone vibrated. The text read, "warning shot. next time, I shoot to kill."

During lunch, Kellyn and David walked to a secluded corner at the back of the school, their fingers almost touching, then pulling away just before the moment of contact. *Oh My God, I think we're really a couple*, they both thought.

"What was it you wanted to show me?" he asked.

Kellyn glanced around. Then, slowly, she unbuttoned her black Top Shop Bandstand coat. Underneath, she wore a Jesus and Mary Chain T-shirt.

"I've got one just like that," he said.

"Not anymore." She grinned.

"You stole my shirt."

"Want it back?"

"It looks better on you."

Kellyn almost blushed at the compliment.

"I thought you hated them," said David.

"Once you get past all the noise, there's something sort of cool about the band of bees." Kellyn leaned back against the wall. "No one ever comes here," she murmured. It took David a second to comprehend he was being given an invitation to kiss her. Then he understood.

Just before their lips met, Kellyn pushed him away.

"What?" he asked. Then he followed her wide eyes.

Five girls stood in front of them. Their eyes obscured by Burberry bucket hats. Their feet covered by Cavalli gladiator sandals. Fake Chanel handbags around their wrists. *The PBG!*

Kellyn looked surprised by their sudden silent appearance.

"I thought we scared you straight," David said. They remained mute.

Weren't there only four of them last time? Kellyn thought, her confusion growing. Then she noticed the fifth PBG had long, thick shiny black hair hanging down from under her hat.

"That's a lovely little clique you've got there, Doodles,"

jeered Kellyn, using Dorinda's hated nickname. "You're the queen of pee."

"Ladies," said Dorinda, "let's show Kellyn the present we've got her."

In unison, four hands dipped into four fake bags. Kellyn grabbed David and pushed him in front of her. Then she peeked over his shoulder. The four PBG pulled their hands out of their bags and held their middle fingers aloft.

"Aren't they the *cutest?*" laughed Dorinda. "Okay, go back to what you were doing. It looks like *so* much fun." Then she snapped her fingers. "*Allons-y!*" she called out. The four PBG trotted obediently after their new leader.

"I'm the one you liked," Kellyn called after them. "*She's* the victim."

The Um Girl bringing up the rear turned back to the shaken Kellyn. "Um . . . we're not the PBG anymore. Now we're the Dorinda Militia." The Um Girl giggled, then ran to catch up with her friends.

"You threw me under the bus," accused David. "The *pee* bus!"

"I was scared," admitted Kellyn.

"The embittered sidekick turns to the dark side." David nodded. "*Classic* . . ."

Kellyn watched her onetime best friend walk away. *She's not the victim anymore*, she thought, and then realized that she was feeling sort of proud.

THIRTEEN

Between the Lines

Meet Ally: AMERICA'S NO. 1 JEN GIRL BLOGS FOR U!

Oh My God, you guys!!!! I cannot even put into words what an honor it is to be America's No. 1 Jen Girl. But seeing as they've given me my own blog here at Jen.com, I guess I'll have to try ☺. Just a month ago, I was an ordinary LA girl. Now, I get 2 run out of school three afternoons a week and work at Jen with the most amazing, friendly, generous, fun, cool people ever! Shout-outs to the heads of the fashion, beauty, photo, and entertainment departments. I'm learning so much from you guys, e.g., what kind of coffee you all like!! Exxxtra-special shout-out 2 our amazingly awesome editor and my brand-new

BFF—BNBFF!—Ms. Pixie Furmanovsky, who's totally been my guardian angel. Thanks 2 her, I got 2 sit in on an editorial meeting! That's right, I got 2 watch all these incredible editors come up with stories and features for our next issue. And I got 2 see Pixie pick and choose the best ones. She's like a machine! In a good way!! And I got 2 put something on the What's Hot List!!!! I couldn't believe it!! Everyone was looking at me. All I could hear was my heart beating in my ears—that's right, I've got a heart in my ears ☺—and then I said, "What about AC/ DC?" (It just popped into my head, but I've come to legit heart them). And nobody said anything, and I thought I was gonna DIE. But then Pixie started singing, "You Shook Me All Night Long," and then everybody joined in! It was awesome! So AC/ DC are on the What's Hot List because of ME! I totally want a cut of their record sales! Just kidding (not really). So what's next for Ally the Intern, I hear u ask. Will I be packing up clothes for photo shoots or working in the accessories closet or interviewing celebs on the red carpet? Whatever it is—and I hope it's #3 ☺—you'll be the first to read about it here.

Xxxxxx,
A
(Tuesday, April 2, 6:20 P.M.)

Alison flushed with pride as she sat in her bedroom and gazed at her first ever *Jen.com* blog entry. *Millions of girls will read that*, she thought. *Millions of girls will read about me and they'll think, If she can get her dream job, maybe I can, too.* Of course, she wasn't telling the whole exact truth. If she had, the big glass building in Century

City would have been besieged by hysterical, demented teenage girls desperate to drop Alison out of a window and step into her shoes.

What she didn't tell her readers was that while working at *Jen* was absolutely Alison's dream job, she wasn't really *working* there. Three afternoons a week, she'd take the elevator up to the twenty-third floor, make her way to Pixie's Palace, and the two girls would order food and drink from Avril Lavigne's publicist. They'd spend the rest of the day dressing up in clothes from the fashion department, filming themselves lip-synching to pop songs, and posting abusive messages on the forum of despised rival magazine *Pink Sugar*. Plus, there were presents. Lots of presents. Alison only had to mention a movie she couldn't wait to see, and an invitation to a screening would show up at the office. The same with DVD box sets. The same with shoes and cosmetics. "Behold the awesome power of *Jen!*" proclaimed Pixie. *I think it's more to do with the awesome power of you*, thought Alison fondly.

As much as Pixie loved to hang out and goof off with Alison, she was still able to devote time to every department, every editor, every story, and every inch of the magazine. She knew everyone's name, she remembered everyone's birthday, and she brought out the best in everyone. She was the perfect boss. Except for *one* time . . .

It was Alison's second week. Cutesy Woo had peeped something about Pixie being in a meeting with advertisers. Alison made her way to the Palace, flopped down on one of the huge comfy cushions, kicked off her shoes, and picked up the latest copy of Italian *Vogue*. Then she'd heard a knock on the door.

"Uh . . . come," she'd said, echoing Pixie's curt command. A studious-looking girl walked cautiously into the office. "Hi," she'd said, "there's no other interns around. If you're not busy, maybe you'd like to help me with something." Alison remembered jumping up from the cushion, overjoyed to be entrusted with any kind of work. The girl was a staff writer who had just finished interviewing people about their worst first dates. Alison had followed the writer into her cubicle. No chandelier. No throne. No cushions. The writer had handed her a digital recorder. "It'd be great if you could transcribe this." Alison remembered feeling tense. "I only really speak a little French. Is this in French? Because I don't really speak any French." The writer had smiled. "Transcribe. It's like taking dictation. Just copy down what everyone says."

"I can do that!" Alison had said. She'd taken a seat at the adjoining cubicle, plugged in a pair of headphones, brought up a new file on the PowerBook, and begun transcribing. Moments later, Alison's yelps of laughter had brought the writer over to her cubicle. "THIS IS HILARIOUS!" Alison had bawled, headphones still in her ears. "I CAN'T WAIT TO READ IT."

Then Pixie had shown up. She'd shoved the writer out of the way and yanked the headphones from Alison's ears. "What do you think you're doing?" she'd demanded. Alison had pointed at the writer. "I was just transcaping her story. It's *so* funny. I was just telling her I can't wait to read it . . ."

Pixie's eyes had seemed to disappear. She'd clenched her fists by her sides. "So she's your friend now. You like her better than me."

Alison remembered how confused she'd felt. She remembered the way the writer stared down at the ground and said nothing. She remembered having to hurry after Pixie and bang repeatedly on the locked Palace door before she was permitted to reenter. She remembered Pixie blaming her bizarre behavior on having to deal with advertisers. Alison didn't remember ever seeing the staff writer again.

Pixie's behavior had been unexpected and unsettling. But everyone has an off day, Alison told herself, everyone gets grouchy. As if to confirm Alison's diagnosis, Pixie wiped away Alison's suspicions by dropping an incredible surprise in her lap.

FOURTEEN
America's Sweetheart

Meet Ally: AMERICA'S NO. 1 *JEN* GIRL BLOGS FOR U!

Oh My God, you guys, guess what? Jen's putting Treasure Spinney on the cover. . . . AND I'M WRITING THE STORY!!!! SERIOUSLY!!! ME!!! I am going 2 the photo shoot at her amazing house in Laurel Canyon. I'll be spending time alone with her, finding out all the inside dirt you guys are desperate to find out. We're totally gonna bond. We've got so much in common: America's No. 1 Jen Girl meets America's No. 1 TV Star!!!! True Confession: I've actually met T-Spin on 2 occasions (Hey, it's LA! Famous people are everywhere: I looked out my window this morning and the first thing I saw was Ryan

Gosling bending down to scoop up dog poo . . . at least I HOPE that's what he was doing ☺). Don't know if she'll remember, but I know we'll have fun catching up. You guys, my dream job just keeps getting better and better . . .

Xxxxxxxxxx,
A
(Thursday, April 18, 5:08 P.M.)

"Something needs to be done about Abigail Breslin!"

The scream of rage was followed by the smashing of glass. The *Jen* team hovered nervously by the front porch of the lovely rustic Laurel Canyon home, where they had arranged to photograph and interview Treasure Spinney. The publicist had confirmed that the cover story on the adorable fourteen-year-old star of the ailing teen drama *Signal Hill* would take place at eleven in the morning. That meant an hour for hair and makeup. Three more hours for the shoot. And a final forty-five-minute Q&A session. When ace reporter Alison Cole showed up outside the house at two o'clock on the dot and saw the *Jen* crew milling around the street, she immediately assumed she'd missed the entire shoot.

"It hasn't started yet," said Amandine the editor responsible for making sure the day ran like clockwork, through gritted teeth. "She only showed up at twelve thirty. And she still hasn't even let us in the house."

A furious shriek from inside the ivy-covered cottage was followed by the sound of more glass breaking.

"And *that's* been happening every five minutes," hissed one of the hair people.

And then the front door creaked open. A small man, whose expression and posture made him seem like he spent his entire life walking barefoot across broken glass, tiptoed out onto the front porch. This was Treasure's manager, Ian Whitley-Bay.

"Treasure's dealing with some devastating news. She was passed over for the role of her life. The title part in *Little Stumpy Girl*. She's *crushed*."

Another scream of "*Breslin!*" was accompanied by the sounds of further destruction.

Ian Whitley-Bay, speaking in hushed tones, informed the staff that his client, though wounded to the core, was still a professional and would do them the favor of continuing with the shoot. "But," he reminded them, "this story is about Tresh merch."

Blank looks.

"This profile is to sell Treasure's *Little Treasure* dolls, her new range of T-Spin sports-and-leisure wear, her fragrance *The Smell of Treasure*, and her upcoming CD *Quite Valuable*. We're not answering any questions about *Signal Hill*. We're transitioning away from TV. Understood?"

The staff nodded their assent. Ian Whitley-Bay ushered them into the house.

Forty minutes later, Treasure had still refused to venture out of the bedroom. She hated the color of the walls in the hallway. "They're eggshell blue," explained Ian Whitley-Bay. "Treasure wants them ecru. It's more peaceful."

More blank looks.

"This isn't *literally* Treasure's house," Ian Whitley-Bay was forced to further explain. "This was the sort of house she thought her fans would like to imagine she lived in."

"As opposed to her actual miserable existence in a rented poolside bungalow in the Chateau Marmont since she got herself legally emancipated from her mother," Alison heard the stylists gossip.

Twenty minutes later, a tense negotiation was taking place between the photo editor, Ian Whitley-Bay, and the actual owners of the property, who didn't seem too excited about having the walls of their hallway painted ecru for the day.

I can help, thought Alison. *I know her. Sort of.* While the negotiations continued and time kept ticking away, Alison wandered quietly upstairs. She came to the closed bedroom door, knocked twice, and then walked in. Treasure Spinney was lying on the four-poster bed. The famous tumbling chestnut curls were hidden under her pink Juicy Couture hoodie. Her face was free of makeup. Her toes were flaked with chipped black nail polish. The TV was on. She was watching herself—her much more vivacious and beautified self—on an old episode of *Signal Hill*.

Alison waited for the actress to notice her. After a moment, she gave up waiting. "Hi," she said. "I'm Alison. I'm with *Jen?* I thought maybe you'd like to talk."

Treasure Spinney stared at her.

"I'm with the magazine," Alison explained again. Treasure kept staring. It suddenly occurred to Alison that Treasure had *completely forgotten that there was anyone in the house.* "Everyone's really excited about the shoot and the story—we're all such big fans," prattled Alison, trying to jog the little star's memory while putting her at ease. "Me especially. We've met before, actually. It was at Barneys. Such a funny story . . ." Alison launched into a heavily censored account of how the pair of them tussled over a Stella McCartney trench coat (a fight that had triggered Alison's firepower, leading her down the path to superherodom).

Treasure kept staring as Alison talked.

"So I've got some questions," Alison continued brightly. "I wrote them down so I wouldn't forget." Alison pulled a notebook and a digital voice recorder from her bag. She set them down on the edge of the bed. "I've never done this before," Alison admitted. Then she cleared her throat and asked, "What's the last thing on your mind when you go to sleep at night?"

Alison smiled encouragingly at Treasure. "I worry that there might be squirrels trapped in the air-conditioning unit," she said, hoping to inspire the blank-faced girl. "I hate them." No response was forthcoming. The ace reporter tried again. "If Ben & Jerry were to give you your own ice cream, what flavor would you want and what would it be called?"

Treasure gazed at Alison's eager face for another moment. Then she spoke. Or rather, *screamed.* "*Stalker! She's trying to hurt me!*"

Seconds later, Ian Whitley-Bay ran in. He sized up the situation and thrust an accusing finger in Alison's face. "What did you say to her?"

Alison was aghast. "Nothing," she gasped. "I asked her about ice cream."

"Don't you see how fragile she is right now?" he said.

The *Jen* team crowded into the bedroom. They also sized up the situation, and they joined Ian Whitley-Bay in regarding Alison with disapproval.

Alison was shocked. "I didn't *do* anything."

Treasure beckoned to Ian Whitley-Bay. He kneeled on the floor as she leaned over and whispered in his ear, all the while fixing her eyes on Alison.

Ian Whitley-Bay's knees creaked as he pulled himself upright. "You frightened her. But because she's the sweetest, most talented girl in the world, she's decided to forgive you."

"Thank you *so* much," gushed Amandine. "She shouldn't really be doing the interview. She's just an intern. She doesn't know how to act."

Traitor! fumed Alison.

Ian Whitley-Bay continued, directing his gaze toward Alison. "Treasure knows you were only trying to help. That's why she trusts you to run a little errand for her."

This is going to be great for my story, Alison thought.

"She'd love for you to go to Sprinkles and pick her up a box of her favorite red-velvet cupcakes and a dolce espresso from Urth Caffé."

Alison flushed with excitement. This was something she could totally do. The high-end cupcake boutique and the organic coffeehouse were regular Beverly Hills haunts of hers and her former friends. Alison felt a wave of sympathy for Treasure. She'd been steamrollered by Abigail Breslin. She wasn't going to get to be Little Stumpy Girl. She needed the sweet comfort of a chocolate cupcake. After she'd eaten her cake and downed her espresso, she'd turn on that star charisma. And Alison would be credited with saving the whole shoot and turning in the best first interview of any ace reporter ever!

"Your wish is my command!" she exclaimed as she rushed out of the bedroom.

As Treasure watched Alison leave, a malicious little twinkle gleamed in her eyes.

FIFTEEN

Hot Cakes

"*You understand* the plan?" said Alison to Designated Dean as he drove the Mercedes back down Laurel Canyon toward Beverly Hills.

Designated Dean grunted.

"Then repeat the plan to me so I know you understand."

Designated Dean gave her an irritated sidelong look. He'd enjoyed a carefree existence living in his parents' garage before David Eels had got him involved with Alison and their bizarre nighttime crime-fighting antics. Now he was at the beck and call of a petulant teenage girl. Still, he got a free car out of the deal. Plus, having to ferry her around meant he couldn't set aside any time to look for a job. So he repeated the plan. Or at least he would have done so, except that once he started thinking about cupcakes, it led him to thinking about Twinkies, which, in turn, made him start thinking about Snickers bars, and then he began wondering about the last time he had a Reese's . . . and then her high, screechy voice broke up his thoughts.

"*The plan* is, you drop me at Sprinkles. Then you go Urth Caffé, pick up the espresso, then come pick me up at the same place you dropped me. Then we head back up to Laurel Canyon. Got it?"

Designated Dean grunted.

"Then tell me the plan so I know you understand."

Designated Dean gave her an irritated sidelong look. Once again, thinking about cupcakes made him think about Ho Hos . . .

Alison jumped out of the Mercedes on Little Santa Monica Boulevard. She watched Designated Dean drive away and tried to convince herself that he had committed the plan to memory. Then she hurried toward the Beverly Hills branch of Sprinkles.

"*Yesss!*" Alison was exuberant.

There had not been a day since its opening that the trendy cupcake store had not attracted lines around the corner. Its high prices, pretty packaging, and proud declaration that it used only the finest ingredients had quickly won a dedicated following, who enjoyed the idea that they were consuming the same sweet substance as Sprinkles boosters like Oprah, Katie Holmes, and Lindsay Lohan. But no one was there today. Not a line outside. Not a huddle around the counter. In fact, there were drapes pulled down over the windows.

Undaunted, Alison gave the door a shove. It was locked. She pushed again. Still locked. *It's not closed. It can't be closed.* She knocked on the glass door. She heard footsteps on the other side. Then the door began to open. She sighed with relief. But the door only opened a crack. Just enough for the girl on the other side to say, "Sorry, we're closed."

Alison couldn't believe what she was hearing. *I need to save the shoot!* "You can't be closed. People need cupcakes!"

The girl didn't open the door any further. "We're being used as a location today. But come back tomorrow. It'll be business as usual."

A location? What kind of madness was this? "But I just need four cakes. Four red-velvet cakes."

"I'm sorry," said the girl again. The crack got smaller. She was closing the door.

Do something! Alison raised her voice and did a very LA thing. "*They're for Treasure Spinney!*" she said.

The door stopped closing. The crack got wider. Alison looked over the girl's shoulder. Cameras. Lights. Models wearing floaty slip dresses, holding cupcakes up to their open mouths but not actually taking bites.

"It's for a magazine," said the girl.

"So's this," replied Alison. "We're doing a *cover story* on *Treasure Spinney* for *Jen* magazine." Once again, Alison spoke in high-volume, LA name-dropper tones. Her loud voice turned the heads of the people working inside the store.

"Did she say she was from *Jen*?" asked one of the photographer's assistants.

"I think she did," confirmed a fashion editor.

"I know who that is!" squealed one of the models. "That's America's No. 1 *Jen* Girl!"

More members of the magazine team began spilling out of the bakery and into the main part of the shop.

"That's the girl who called us boring and then set us on fire!" yelled a writer. And that's when Alison saw Sprinkles was filled with an angry mob, everyone sporting a *Pink Sugar* T-shirt.

"You're a long way from home, *Jen* Girl," said the fashion editor, a dangerous glint in her eyes. "You looking to defect?"

"I'm looking for cakes, that's all," Alison replied, noticing the same dangerous glint in the eyes of all the *Pink Sugar* staffers.

"You're on our turf now, munchkin," said the *Pink Sugar* fashion editor in low, threatening tones. "This could play out one of two ways. You could beg us pretty please for your fancy cakes, and maybe we might take pity on you. Or you could keep acting like you think you're something special, and you'll get the door slammed in your face. What's it gonna be? I'm waiting." The *Pink Sugar* fashion editor locked her eyes with Alison. She picked up a Madagascar bourbon-vanilla cake and tossed it up and down in her palm. Every time it plopped back down on her hand, a small cloud of sugar wafted into the air.

Alison felt her mouth go dry.

The rest of the *Pink Sugar* staff picked up cupcakes and fell into rhythm with the fashion editor. They tossed the cakes up and down in their hands. The models didn't join in the cake tossing, but they inched closer to the staff members so they could inhale the clouds of sugar.

"*All right!*" blurted Alison. "I think *Pink Sugar* is a really, really good magazine. If you'd had an intern contest, I'd probably have entered that and set *Jen* on fire." *Forgive me, Jen*, she thought. "So can I please, please have four red-velvet cakes? *Please.*"

The fashion editor stopped tossing the cupcake in the air. She kept her eyes on Alison but spoke to the *Pink Sugar* troops assembled behind her. "What do you say, *Pink Sugar*, do we let the *Jen* girl have her cakes?"

There was a long tense silence. Then an accessories intern yelled, "Let her have it!"

Uh-oh, thought Alison.

Splat! A spiced ginger-lemon cake with cream-cheese frosting hit her full in the face. Alison gasped in shock.

Squish! A chocolate-chip-studded peanut-butter cake with fudge filling smashed into her hair and began dribbling down her forehead.

Alison stumbled blindly as a rainbow of flavors slammed into her face and body. She tried to scream, but her mouth kept filling with hurled cupcake fragments. She started to back out of the store but slipped on a discarded slice of banana cake.

The laughter from the *Pink Sugar* mob rang in her ears. She felt her fingertips catch fire. Alison shot an arm out and caught the next cupcake missile aimed her way. It was a walnut-studded carrot cake. She sent a wave of heat running through it and then leapt to her feet and threw it back into the crowd of *Pink Sugar* staffers. Cupcake residue still clogged her eyes. She couldn't see the enemy, but she could hear someone scream, "That *burned!*" The hail of cakes headed at her was blurry, but Alison suddenly felt like her senses had become heightened under pressure. She reached out and caught a pumpkin cake, shot it back at her attackers and, once again, heard the shriek of pain.

Alison blinked the last pieces of cupcake out of her eyes. Now she was the one staring down the *Pink Sugar* fashion editor.

"There's one of me," said Alison, "and there's all of you. Doesn't seem like a fair fight, does it?" The *Pink Sugar* girl tried to stand her ground. "Maybe you should call some friends," suggested Alison. Some anonymous coward threw a strawberry cake. Never taking her eyes away from the *Pink Sugar* girl's face, Alison reached out a hand and caught the cake. Then she applied a little heat, hurled it back into the crowd, and waited until she heard the anonymous coward scream in pain. The *Pink Sugar* girl gulped. Then she turned around and ran for the bakery at the back of the store.

Two seconds later, the rest of the *Pink Sugar* staff and models were scrambling over each other to follow her. The bakery door slammed shut. Alison made her way across the cupcake-covered floor. She knocked politely on the locked door. "So can I please, please have four red-velvet cakes. *Please?*"

Alison touched a hand to her hair and pulled back a chunk of chocolate. *What do I look like?* she wondered. But just as she was about to look for a reflective surface that wasn't splattered with cupcake, the bakery door opened. A box slid out. Alison peeked inside. Four red-velvet cupcakes.

"Thanks, you guys. We should totally have an inter-magazine softball game. Tell me what date works for you. Bye now . . ." Alison made her way out of the shop and rushed out into the street, where Designated Dean was *not* waiting for her.

I knew he didn't understand the plan, she seethed.

SIXTEEN
Nick of Time

$\mathcal{T}he$ $\mathbf{cab}$ $\mathbf{started}$ to slow down, but as the driver got a look at the cupcake-coated Alison, he picked up speed and drove away.

"It's made from the finest ingredients," she screamed after him. She checked her watch. Five fifteen.

Alison tore down Wilshire Boulevard, charged across the road, and made her way through Beverly Drive. She approached Urth Caffé, where she saw no sign of Designated Dean. (Meanwhile Double D sat in the Mercedes outside a 7-Eleven on Olympic Boulevard. He had a hunch that there was somewhere he was supposed to be. But, as he'd just gulped down his sixth consecutive Baby Ruth and gone into sugar shock, the hunch quickly vanished.)

Breathless and disheveled, Alison stumbled into the tranquility of Urth Caffé. Every head turned. All the models and actresses, who sat nursing their post-yoga Antigua Sumatra javas, gaped at her. Alison took her place at the back of the line and tried to act like she didn't know she was the object of attention. Which was difficult as pieces of cupcake continued to fall out of her hair and ears. And then it got even harder. Lark Rise, who looked like she'd just showered under a rain forest waterfall and been dried by the warmth of the sun, approached her, eyes welling over with sympathy.

"Oh, you poor thing," Lark said softly. "Is there anything I can do to help? Do you need money or somewhere to stay?" Then her eyebrows shot up in shocked recognition. "Alison? Oh My God!" Lark's sympathy quickly vanished to be replaced by stifled laughter.

At least this can't get any worse, Alison assured herself.

"T!" called out Lark. "Look who it is!"

"What *happened?*" said T, jumping up from the table, where he and Lark had been discussing mature business.

Alison gave her boyfriend a beseeching *"Please, can we not talk about this?"* look and simply said, "I'm working."

Lark smiled brightly. "T told me you were interning at *Jen*. That's so wonderful for you. My little sister and all her friends love that magazine. You must be like a queen to the under-tens." Lark shot T a conspiratorial smirk. He didn't smirk back. Undaunted, Lark continued, "Do you want me to take you to the little girls' room and help get you nice and clean?"

The Urth Caffé barista gestured to Alison that he was ready to take her order. "You guys, go back to your meeting," Alison told T and Lark.

"She's a riot." Lark laughed as they left Alison to pick up her espresso.

Five minutes later, Alison was back on the street, juggling the red-velvet cupcake box, the espresso cup, and her iPhone. The Hottiemobile was nowhere to be seen. "The plan," she yelled into the phone. "You forgot the plan!"

Suddenly, a hand took the cupcake box and the coffee from her grasp. It was T. "Come on," he said.

T had just done three things that had given him Permanent Boyfriend Immunity: (1) He had come to Alison's rescue in her moment of need. (2) He had totally abandoned Lark Rise to rush after Alison and offer to drive her back to Laurel Canyon. (3) He was confessing how much he had come to loathe Lark Rise.

"It's all about *her*," T said as he drove the Chevy Impala up the twisting road. "That whole thing about wanting to start an alternative to the school paper? What she really wanted was a staff of lackeys who would help her put together her own paper."

"Like *O*, only *L*?" said Alison.

"Probably." T shrugged. "And she was mean to you."

"Was she being mean, though?" asked Alison, loving every second of this. "Or was she just being *mature*?"

T grinned. "There's no way you'll ever let me forget that, is there?"

Alison felt a warm glow of happiness. *We're back in the groove*, she thought, and resolved to write Lark Rise a nice thank-you note.

T pulled up outside Pixie's non-home. "Want me to wait for you?" he asked.

She shook her head no. "I'll ride back with the *Jen* crew," she said, and leaned in to kiss him goodbye.

"You taste good," he said, licking powdered sugar from his lips.

Alison skipped into the cottage. Lights and camera equipment were everywhere.

"Jesus God," yelped Amandine, catching sight of the cake-stained Alison. "What happened? Where have you been?"

Alison brandished the cupcake package and the coffee cup. Amandine clutched her heart in relief and began to walk Alison up the cottage stairs to the bedroom. "She's been an angel. Totally cooperative. Sat through hair and makeup without complaining. And she looks *amazing*. There's a chance we can get this done and be out of here before midnight."

Ian Whitley-Bay stood at the top of the stairs. "Hurry, hurry," he chirped, clapping his hands. "She's *dying*."

Alison went to hand the box and the cup to Treasure's manager. He shook his head. "She wants *you*. She was insistent. 'Have the girl bring the goodies,' she said."

Amandine went to pat Alison on the head, then drew back when she saw the chocolate caked in her hair. "She's America's No. 1 *Jen* Girl, you know," Amandine proudly informed Ian Whitley-Bay.

He knocked twice on the bedroom door. "Treasure, darling, she's here." He pushed the door open.

Alison walked into the cottage bedroom. She heard the

door snap shut behind her. Treasure was standing by the window. Alison couldn't help but gasp when she turned around. The hair people had made Treasure's chestnut curls fall about her face and shoulders in delicate waves. The makeup people had added depth and mystery to her angelic features. She wore a long flowing white-silk dress. A clothes rail on the other side of the room carried a spotless selection of items from her T-Spin sports-and-leisure-wear collection. "You look *so* incredible," breathed Alison. "This is going to be the best cover ever."

"Until you ruined it," said Treasure.

Alison looked baffled.

Treasure reached for the cupcake box, opened it, and selected a red-velvet cake. Then she winked at Alison and smeared the chocolate over her immaculate makeup and down her white-silk dress. "We could be twins." She smiled at the stunned Alison. Then she snatched the espresso cup and tossed the contents over the brand-new clothes on the rail. And, finally, she *screamed* . . .

"*That girl's gone crazy!*"

"Oh My God, Alison, what happened?" gasped Cutesy Woo as Alison stomped furiously out of the elevator on the twenty-third floor and through the *Jen* reception area.

Some of the other editors poked their heads out of their offices. Word had spread that the Treasure Spinney shoot was running *hours* late. And that it was Alison's fault. Alison ignored all the questioning and accusing glances. She kicked open the door of Pixie's Palace. Her friend was sitting behind her throne.

"Allywally," said Pixie, shocked at Alison's appearance. "I heard something happened, but I don't . . ." She didn't get a chance to finish the sentence. Alison walked up to her glittery desk, kicking huge fluffy pillows out of the way. Her eyes were red with rage. Her voice was shaking with anger.

"*I hate Treasure Spinney,*" she spat. "*I want her on the What's Not List.*"

SEVENTEEN
Buried Treasure

The following Monday in the BHHS *cafeteria . . .*

Bianca White screeched with laughter. The student who saw her acting career nipped in the bud when Treasure Spinney had her kicked off *Signal Hill* held up her BlackBerry so her small group of followers could get a good look. The message was from one of her old friends on the *SH* crew. The set was buzzing with the rumor that Treasure's Little Treasure dolls were being removed from shelves because of their high lead content.

"I knew she was toxic," crowed Bianca.

Tuesday in the BHHS cafeteria . . .

It wasn't just Kellyn's scarlet American Apparel headband

that made her feel like Snow White. She looked around the table at her new lunchmates. The guy with the tiny head. The one with the phlegm problems. The guy who used to have a horrifying toenail. And the one called Odor Eater. When Kellyn had first demanded that David introduce her to his friends, her motive was to make him see the horror she had rescued him from (and, by extension, let him know what he'd be going back to if he ever got out of line). But, unbelievably, Kellyn found that she sort of *liked* hanging out with these misfits. They accorded her instant Queen Bee status. They took her advice on grooming and clothing and not talking with their mouths full of food. In return, they introduced her to a whole world of comics and games and music and movies, almost all of which seemed to feature teenage Japanese schoolgirls clutching machine guns.

Kellyn's lunchtime companions even attempted to immerse themselves in *her* interests. Which is how Tiny Head came to bring up the reports that Treasure Spinney's T-Spin line had been removed from retail outlets after it had been revealed that the clothes were manufactured in sweatshops.

"That's so interesting, *Bruce*," Kellyn told Tiny Head. "Why can't *you* let me know about important world events like that?" she chided David. He hung his head. Kellyn showed him no favor in public, but underneath the lunch table, their fingers were intertwined.

Wednesday in the BHHS cafeteria . . .

"Um . . . did you guys see that Treasure Spinney's CD isn't coming out?" inquired The Um Girl.

"Oh, no," said Dorinda. "I can't believe we're being deprived of another singing actress."

"I know," agreed Infected Nose Ring. "It sucks. I bet she was awesome."

Dorinda gave the girl a weary look.

"Right," Infected Nose Ring nodded. "You were joking. She probably can't sing at all. That's why they're not putting it out."

"I knew she was joking," piped up Pink Glitter Eye Shadow.

"You're *so* funny and *so* smart," gushed Too Long In The Tanning Booth. "We'd still be throwing pee at people if it wasn't for you."

Dorinda surveyed her adoring acolytes. They dressed like her. They hung on her every word. "*Mon Dieu*." she said under her breath.

Thursday in the BHHS cafeteria . . .

Everyone in the cafeteria had the clip on their phones. The tearful host of *Good Day LA* showed the film of her Siamese cat projectile vomiting. "This makes cats sick, and I will *never* wear it *again*," she sobbed, holding up the perfume bottle whose label read *The Smell of Treasure*. "And if you love your pets, you won't wear it, either." She wagged a finger at the camera. "Shame on you, Treasure Spinney. . . ."

Everyone in the cafeteria wagged their fingers in sympathy.

Friday in the BHHS cafeteria . . .

"I can't believe how fast some things happen," marveled T. "It was, like, a week ago, I was driving you up to Treasure Spinney's big cover shoot, and now her show's *canceled*."

"You don't mess with the Hottie," joked Alison. Last week seemed a long way away. She remembered her fury at the way

Treasure Spinney had treated her. But then she remembered Pixie reminding her, "You're under my wing. Nothing bad's going to happen to you while we're friends." She remembered how much that had comforted her. A friend like Pixie was way more important than an irritant like Treasure Spinney. Her rage quickly abated and she was able to laugh about the incident with her sympathetic *Jen* friends.

"I guess she's not gonna be on your cover anymore," said T.

"Guess not," muttered Alison. But she didn't really care that much. She was more concerned with the fact that she was sitting with T, while Kellyn sat with David and his friends and Dorinda occupied a table with her adoring entourage. *I guess we all found better friends*, she thought.

A thunderous church bell rang four times. It was the intro to AC/DC's "Hell's Bells," which was now Alison's ringtone.

T laughed out loud. "You've never known the name of any singer or group ever. But suddenly you're a fan."

"I commit fully to the rock," she said proudly. Then she looked at her iPhone. Pixie's cute smiling face. She read the text, then said, "What am I doing this weekend? Do I wanna come over to her place Saturday?"

T frowned. "Saturday? As in Saturday when we were gonna go up to Runyon Canyon?"

Alison gave T an apologetic look.

"But you'd rather hang out with her?" he asked.

Alison nodded.

"Even though you see her all the time at the magazine?" he went on.

Alison nodded again. "She's been so good to me," she said,

hoping he'd understand. "She's so inspiring. *And* she's so much fun. How do you get to be inspiring *and* fun without being a cartoon character? And the fact that she's asked me to her house. To spend the weekend with her. I can't pass that up, T. I just can't. Runyon Canyon will always be there. Unless there's an earthquake. But that won't happen this weekend. And if it does, aren't you glad I'll be safe at Pixie's house instead of buried under rocks?" She gave him an appealing look.

T had no arguments to counter her look or her logic. "Another time," he agreed. Bursting with sudden excitement, she texted Pixie back the word *Yes*.

EIGHTEEN
Alison in Wonderland

Alison knew that Pixie lived somewhere in Malibu. She hadn't realized her friend lived in *all of Malibu*. As the limo Pixie sent to pick her up waited for the iron doors to creak all the way open, Alison got her first glimpse at the mansion that was to be the weekend's home away from home.

Alison lived in a big house in Brentwood. Kellyn lived in a big house in the Hollywood Hills. T lived in a big house in Los Feliz. Dorinda lived in a big house in Beverly Hills. Pixie's place could have fit all these big houses under its huge roof and still have made room for a indoor football arena.

As the car made its way up the driveway, passing the lushly attended lawns, Alison saw a small dot in the doorway of the Georgian-style mansion. It was Pixie. She was jumping up and down with excitement. The car hadn't fully come to a halt before Pixie pulled open the door and began to drag Alison out.

"I'm pleased to see you, too," spluttered Alison. "But you don't have to lick me." Then she saw that the tongue lapping at her cheek belonged to the dog Pixie held in her arm.

"It's Little Pixie!" she exclaimed. "My Maltipoo. You can hold him while I show you around." The dog flew into Alison's arms as Pixie grabbed a handful of her T-shirt and pulled her into the house.

Sixteen bedrooms, twelve bathrooms with gold-plated sunken baths, ten hand-carved fireplaces, two guesthouses, one swimming pool, a conservatory, a massage room, a wine cellar, a gym, a screening room, and a basketball court later, Pixie walked a luxury-overloaded Alison to the bedroom they'd be sharing over the weekend.

"I need to leave a trail of salt behind me. Otherwise I'll get lost in the night, and no one will ever find me again," said Alison.

"You'll get used to it," predicted Pixie. "Next time you come, you'll be acting like it's your other home. Which I want it to be." Pixie gave Alison's arm a friendly squeeze. Little Pixie licked her face. Pixie reached for the dog. "Come back to Mommy now."

The Maltipoo gripped Alison's arm tighter and shrank away from Pixie. "Take him," Alison pleaded, but the dog showed no inclination to go back to its owner.

"He likes you better than me," noted Pixie.

As they approached her bedroom, the door opened and a maid exited.

"Pilar!" squealed Pixie. The maid froze outside the door, her eyes on the floor. "Pilar, this is my friend, Alison. She's staying for the weekend."

The maid nodded.

"So I guess you're going to pick up Perdita from her grandma now?"

The maid mumbled, "Yes, Miss Pixie."

Pixie smiled at Alison. "That's her little girl. *So* cute." She turned back to the maid. "You give her a kiss from me. And bring her to visit again. We had fun the last time she was here."

The maid nodded one last time and attempted to melt into the wall as Pixie led Alison into her bedroom.

"*Hello . . . hello . . .*" Alison heard her voice echo around the bedroom, which was Pixie's office blown up to three thousand square feet. The same candy-striped wallpaper. The same chandelier. A two-hundred-inch plasma screen. And a bed that looked big enough to provide sleeping space for the entire *Jen* staff, plus all the people from the twenty-two floors below. Pixie pointed her phone at the windows. They slid open, revealing a massive balcony, which had its own pool, hot tub, and sun loungers. It also had a servant who was fluffing up towels and laying out robes, one of which, Alison noted, had her initials on it.

"Wow" she said. And, at the same time, she thought, *Now I have to have Pixie over to my house. I need to get a new house.*

Pixie beamed at Alison's awed reaction. "So what do you wanna do first?" she said.

Alison couldn't wait to jump into the pool, but Pixie had a better idea. Bursting with excitement, Pixie pulled Alison and

Little Pixie away from the balcony and the inviting-looking pool. "This is the funniest thing *ever!*"

Alison followed her hostess down a flight of stairs and then into a dimly lit corridor. Pixie stopped, turned a key, and an old oak door opened up to reveal a vast library filled with leather-bound books.

"Old books. My absolute favorite things," said Alison, attempting to sound enthralled.

"Just wait," insisted Pixie. She led Alison to a heavy velvet curtain, drew it back, and gestured to another door. Little Pixie trembled in Alison's arm. Alison shared the dog's trepidation. Pixie opened the hidden door with a flourish. Inside was a small cramped room dominated by a wall of video monitors.

"Our security system is *awesome*," Pixie gloated.

Alison looked at the screens: slightly blurred images, mostly of servants. Alison felt a little let down. She *really* wanted to be in that pool. She couldn't *wait* to feel the fluffy monogrammed robe around her. Pixie sensed that she was losing her audience's attention.

"But that's not all we can do. Look, there's Pilar!" Pixie pointed to the monitor showing the silent maid changing out of her work clothes.

"She can't wait to see her little girl." Pixie smiled. Then she touched a button on the control panel under the screens. "Now watch this," she said, almost under her breath.

Suddenly, Pilar's image filled every screen. The maid picked up her bag, went to open the door. The multiple screens showed the maid pulling at the door and then looking baffled.

"She can't understand it." Pixie laughed. "How does *thees* keep happening to me?" she added, adopting a broad Mexican accent. "She doesn't get that I can control all the locks from in here."

Alison stared at the multiple screens. The maid was getting increasingly frustrated. She was banging at the door and calling out soundlessly for help.

"Help! Help!" mocked Pixie. Pixie searched Alison's face for a reaction. Alison knew she was supposed to be laughing, knew she was supposed to be relishing her role as wicked co-conspirator, but she could barely push her face into a smile.

"Maybe you should let her out," suggested Alison, trying to remain calm.

Pixie grinned at Alison. "I will in a minute. She always falls for it."

Alison stared at her friend. "Pixie, it's not funny. She's scared. Let her out."

Pixie rolled her eyes. "God, Alison, it was just a *joke*. Like your stupid red stewardess uniform."

Alison searched Pixie's features for signs of a smile. Or at least some small indication that she was joking. But unless Pixie was a brilliantly accomplished deadpan comedienne, there was nothing but coldness and disdain in her face. *But you said you liked my uniform*, thought Alison, confused. The caustic turn in Pixie's voice caused Little Pixie to squirm in Alison's arms. Suddenly, the hidden surveillance room was feeling extremely claustrophobic.

Sucking air through her teeth to register her displeasure, Pixie touched another button on the control panel. On the screens, multiple Pilars finally managed to open the doors.

"Okay, Buzzkillison, let's go study the Bible. Obviously, *that's* your idea of fun," Pixie sulked. She walked out of the surveillance room.

Everybody has an off day, Alison reminded herself. *Everybody gets grouchy.* Rationalizing further, Alison thought about the incredible pressure Pixie was under as the figurehead of a national magazine. *She carries so much on these skinny shoulders. It's a miracle she's not a million times meaner.* Alison followed, nervously.

As they left, Pilar looked directly into the cameras with hatred burning in her eyes.

But just as quickly and unexpectedly as it had appeared, Pixie's sour mood vanished.

"Okay," she suddenly yelped. "Break over. Back to having fun!"

Ten minutes later, Alison and Pixie were splashing happily in the balcony pool, the weirdness in the surveillance room forgotten. Twenty minutes after that, they were lying on the sun loungers, snuggled in their fluffy robes, as the balcony servant delivered Green Tea Pinkberries with cookies and cream.

Fifteen minutes later, Alison was relaxing in the sun, a smile of satisfaction on her face. *Maybe I could just live here forever*, she thought, *right here on the balcony. I wouldn't even have to move into the house.* The sound of a car coming up the driveway didn't interrupt her thoughts. The sound of Pixie shrieking "Daddy!" did.

There he was, striding into the hallway of the mansion. The guy from the framed photos in Pixie's Palace. Ludovic Furmanovsky. Six foot five. Ramrod-straight posture. Dark hair cut short. Black Armani suit. *Powerful guy*, Alison thought. Then she watched, smiling, as Pixie flew past her and jumped into his arms. *Now watch him melt into a pile of mush.* But he didn't.

Not exactly. Pixie's father accepted the excited embrace from his daughter, but he didn't display the same outpouring of emotions that flooded from her. *Maybe he shows it in different ways,* thought Alison.

Pixie's father reached inside the Armani jacket and pulled out a black laminated plastic rectangle. "New York Fashion Week. All Access," he said.

Pixie stared at the card, held out her hand, then waggled her fingers at Alison, who dutifully scurried up to join her.

"Daddy, this is my best friend Alison. Remember, I told you all about her. She's America's No. 1 *Jen* Girl. She totally makes work fun. Allywally, this is my daddy, who should have told me he was coming back today. But I'll forgive him this time, because he got me something nice."

"Hello, Mr. Furmanovsky," said Alison politely. "You have a beautiful abode." *Abode!* Alison cringed. *Why didn't you just say house? You've never even heard the word abode before.*

Pixie's father gave Alison the vaguest hint of a glance. Then he said, "Get me another Fashion Week pass."

Alison looked confused. "Me? You want me to get you one?"

Pixie punched Alison on the arm and pointed at her father's ear. "Earpiece, you bizarre human." She smiled.

"Oh. Oh, you're getting an All-Access pass for *me*. Oh My God, thank you so much!"

Pixie grabbed Alison. They screamed and jumped up and down. "New York in the fall. Daddy has a penthouse in Trump Tower. We get to go to all the shows and all the after-parties."

Pixie's dad cut in, "I think it's only good for the shows. I'm not sure it gets you into the parties."

The black rectangle hit Pixie's dad on the cheek.

"Then what good is it to me?" Pixie snapped. "*God*, Daddy. *Think*." The Incredible Sulk was back. She dug her nails into Alison's arm. "Come on, Alison." Pixie pulled her toward the staircase. "We're hanging out," she called over her shoulder. "Don't bother us anymore."

As they walked up the steps, Pixie whispered, "Two days from now, we'll be *walking* in the shows. We'll be modeling Marc Jacob's next spring collection. Bet." Then she broke into a run. "Come on, Ally, I know what we can do that'll be the funnest thing *ever*."

Pixie's mood had swung toward manic. Her heart-shaped face was red with the effort of dragging the mattress from the guest-room bed. Alison reluctantly helped her push the mattress out of the room and down the corridor toward the staircase.

"Daddy, look at me!" Pixie screamed as she sledded the mattress down the grand mahogany staircase. But before the mattress reached the ground below, both girls could hear the sound of Pixie's father's car as it drove away from the house. Pixie sprawled on the ground and lay there, not moving, not speaking.

Alison ran down the steps. "Are you okay?" she asked.

Pixie looked up at Alison. "It's your fault he left."

"I've got to get out of here," Alison told her reflection as she stood in one of the mansion's twelve bathrooms. She'd been hiding for almost twenty minutes. "Pixie's a psycho."

Alison's reflection shook her head sadly and presented an alternative viewpoint. "She's a lost lonely girl whose father gives her anything she wants except the one thing she really needs."

"I know *that*," hissed Alison to her reflection. "But I feel weird and awkward, and I can't spend a whole weekend here."

Alison's reflection gave her a reproachful look. "So you're just gonna run away? You could spend the weekend talking to her, *listening* to her, letting her know that you're there for her. But instead, you're choosing to abandon her. Don't you think that makes you worse than her father?"

Alison nodded at her reflection. "You have a point," she conceded. "But, the *whole* weekend?"

Reluctantly, Alison left the bathroom and, after walking down the long, second-floor corridor, realized that she had no idea where she was. *I really should have left a trail of salt!* Too embarrassed to call Pixie's name or wait for a servant to come to her aid, Alison threw open the next door she passed. She looked inside. It was a nondescript living room. Pictures of Pixie covered the walls. A preteen Pixie with a kind-looking woman Alison assumed was her mother. Pixie nuzzling a Chihuahua. Pixie playing on the beach with a Labrador. Pixie squeezing a little wiener dog into a little wiener dog T-shirt. *Cute.* Alison smiled. Then she realized that Pixie was playing with a different dog in every single picture.

Suddenly, she had an inkling of why Little Pixie clung to her. Alison left the living room and tried the next door. Nothing. A blindingly white but otherwise empty room. Something about the room's untouched pristine perfection gave Alison the creeps. She pulled the door shut and hurried down the hallway. One more door lay ahead of her. She opened it cautiously. It was an elevator. *It'll take me back downstairs, and I can yell for help*, she decided. But when the elevator doors opened, Alison found herself on a lower level. She stared at the wood paneling and the red-velvet carpet and the imposing double doors at the end of the corridor. *The longer I'm lost, the more time I get to spend away from Pixie.* Alison made her way toward the doors. She took a breath and then went to push them open.

"What are you doing?" said Pixie.

Alison let out a squeak of fright. She turned to see Pixie standing behind her, arms folded, a cold accusing look in her eyes.

"I got lost," Alison said.

Pixie walked past her and stood against the doors.

"What's in there?" Alison asked.

"What, are you writing a report for *InStyle?*" replied Pixie nastily.

"Maybe I am." Alison smiled, trying not to be drawn into a fight.

"Like they'd want you," Pixie sniffed, walking back down the corridor and *snapping her finger* at Alison to follow. "You might get to see inside at my sweet sixteen. *If* I decide to invite you. I showed your picture to all the hot guys I know. None of them seem to like you. They all like me."

Oh, I am so abandoning you, decided Alison. And then she started coughing.

Ten minutes later, Alison was standing in the driveway of Pixie's mansion, waiting for the driver to bring the car around. Pixie's face was like thunder. Alison kept coughing.

"I"—*cough*—"think I'm"—*cough*—"coming down with something, and I"—*cough*—"couldn't live with myself if you"—*cough*—"caught it, too. Not after you've"—*cough*—"been so"—*cough*—"nice to me."

Alison knew Pixie knew she was lying. Alison felt guilty about lying. But all the guilt in the world amounted to nothing next to the prospect of having to spend the rest of the weekend with Pixie.

The car appeared. The driver held the door open.

"Thank you *so* much," gushed Alison. "This was *so* sweet of you."

"Your cough's getting better," observed Pixie.

Alison broke into a wheezing, spluttering fit. Pixie shook her head and started to walk away. Little Pixie shot straight past her. The Maltipoo scampered across the driveway and hurled itself into Alison's arms, aiming its tongue at her face. Alison tried to detach the dog from her face and hand it back to its owner. Pixie kept her arms folded.

"It's got your germs now. You keep it."

Alison looked shocked. "I can't take your dog."

Pixie curled a lip. "I'm over it. If you don't take it, I'll have the driver leave it in the road."

Alison curled her arm around the dog. "I'm not keeping it. I'm just looking after it for you."

"Do what you want." Pixie shrugged. "It shits on everything. Just like you." And with that, Pixie disappeared back into the mansion.

NINETEEN
Return of the Living Dad

"*Your six o'clock* appointment's here, Mr. Cole. Some girl who says she used to know you."

Roger Cole, the high-powered defense attorney, looked up from his case notes. The suspicion on his face was replaced by surprise when he saw Alison standing in the doorway of his office. She was clutching a tiny dog and a plastic bag.

"I thought you might be hungry," she said.

"So you brought a dog?"

"I brought Koo Koo Roo!" she replied, holding the bag aloft.

This might have been a mistake, thought Alison, dismayed by the way her father continued to look at her from behind his desk. But she couldn't stop thinking about Pixie and her distant dad. *That can't happen to me.* So she had Pixie's driver make two stops.

One at the Koo Koo Roo. And then at the Wilshire Boulevard offices of Yarborough Cole McNabb, Attorneys-at-Law. Where she watched Roger making a small neat pile of his papers. Then he pushed them to one side and gestured hungrily for Alison to get over to his desk. United by their love of poultry, the briefly estranged father and daughter tore open containers and divided up paper napkins and plastic forks.

Alison dropped a morsel of chicken into her newly adopted dog's open mouth.

"If that thing makes a mess in here, you're cleaning it up," warned Roger.

"That *thing* is called Young Angus, and he's never made a mess in the three months I've owned him. Have you found any of his little poo gifts around the house?"

Roger peered at the Maltipoo. "No," he admitted, "I haven't."

"That's because I just got him today!" yelled Alison. "It shouldn't be this easy to lie to you! It wouldn't be if you took an interest, if you ever asked me anything, if you were home more . . ."

Roger looked stunned by her outburst. Alison made an effort to stay calm. *Don't be Pixie*, she warned herself.

"I just think . . ." she began, "It's six o'clock on a Saturday night. Neither of us should be here."

"I have to work," said Roger. But then he did something that had rarely happened in the plush offices of Yarborough Cole McNabb, Attorneys-at-Law. He said, "I'm sorry, you're right." His face softening, he continued, "I'm sorry you have to bring me fast food as an excuse to remind me that you exist. It's not what I want."

I'm sorry, too, Alison wished she could say. *I'm sorry I had to wipe out your ex-wife, but she was about to drop you off a museum roof, and I had to make the choice. I'm sorry I'm the reason you're so sad.* But she couldn't say that, so she said, "I miss having you around to talk to. There are times when I really need you. If you could just say goodbye before you leave for work in the morning. That would be something."

Roger shook his head. "That's *nothing*. From now on, I'm driving you to school every morning. And we're going to eat dinner together at least two nights a week. And we're going to find an activity we can do together. Maybe learn Italian. Or take up sailing . . ."

Alison looked panicked. "Okay, that's *too* much interest."

"That's how I do it." Roger grinned. "With me, it's either all or nothing." And then he broke into a deliberately off-key rendition of the early '90s O-Town ballad "All or Nothing."

Alison covered Young Angus's ears. "Dad, *stop*," she begged.

"What's wrong?" he teased. "You used to *love* O-Town. You watched their show. You had their posters . . ."

"I did not," she shrieked, mortified, but also appreciative of the fact that he was trying to embarrass her. He only did that when he was in a good mood. *We're back in the groove.*

TWENTY

Home Alone

$\mathcal{P}ixie$ sat $alone$ in the middle of her fifty-seat screening room watching *Spastic Surgeon: 3-D*. Even though the yet-to-be-released film had been described as the ultimate grueling experience in edge-of-your-seat horror, no screams emerged from Pixie's mouth. It would have been different if Alison had been there. *As planned*. They'd have screeched and jeered at the film's dumb, obvious scares and clumsy kills. They'd have stuffed themselves full of Dale and Thomas gourmet popcorn. They'd have laughed themselves to sleep. The next day, Pixie would have blindfolded Alison and guided her out to the stables.

She'd have pulled off the blindfold and shown Alison the two gorgeous palomino pintos and told her to choose the one she wanted. Alison would have been in tears over the unexpected, unbelievable gift. "I can't. It's too much. No one's *ever* done anything like this for me before," she would have sobbed. But after she'd spent some time in the saddle, she'd have fallen in love with her new pony. She'd have hugged Pixie tightly and thanked her for the best, the most amazing, most wonderful weekend of her life. And she'd have headed home counting the days until she'd be invited back. That's how the weekend *should* have played out. But, because Alison was ungrateful and stupid and scared and weird; Pixie was alone in an empty screening room staring at a desperately un-scary movie at eight fifteen on a Saturday night.

Pulling her eyes away from the screen, Pixie used her *pixie*Phone to check the Facebook statuses of her *Jen* friends. Amandine was rehearsing with her a cappella group. Waris was at a birthday party. Elspeth had gone bowling! In her wheelchair! Pixie sighed heavily. She'd hired them because they'd all seemed like the sort of girls who would be free every Saturday night and always at her beck and call. But they all had things to do and people to do them with. She knew she could easily pick up the phone and have them scrambling back to the office. She barely even needed an excuse. She could hang out with the kitchen staff like she did when she was younger. She could bring Pilar back, make her watch the movie and eat popcorn. *But she wouldn't be here because she* wants *to spend time with me*, Pixie thought.

She opened the door to what had been her parents' master bedroom. *If Alison hadn't disappointed me and abandoned me, I wouldn't be here*, Pixie thought as she lay down on top of her parents' bed and stared up at the ceiling. Her self-pity floodgates burst open. *No one loves me. No one cares about me. No one is more alone than me.* And then she remembered there were a whole group of people more unloved and more alone than her. A whole group of people who never saw the sun.

TWENTY-ONE

Three of Hearts

$David$ had $been$ surprised when Kellyn texted him late Saturday afternoon to change the location of their date that night to the Beverly Hills branch of family-fun restaurant the Cheesecake Factory. He had been surprised again when, after sitting alone for more than fifteen minutes, Dorinda showed up and sat down opposite him without a word of explanation. He received his third surprise when she pulled out a pack of playing cards, held them in front of him, and said, "Take a card."

Although David couldn't actually identify the Garnier Fructis Sleek & Shine that made Dorinda's hair so lustrous or the Lipstick Queen Black Tie Optional that made her lips so dark and full, he was aware that she looked good and she smelled good. These two facts compelled him to pull a seven of clubs from the middle of the pack she proffered.

"The seven of clubs," she intoned. "That's your choice? You're sticking with that?"

David, unsure of the odd turn this, the first actual date of his life, had taken, nodded.

Dorinda held the pack inches from David's face. "Put it back. Anywhere. Take all the time you need. We've got all night."

With growing trepidation, David replaced the card in the middle of the pack.

Dorinda shuffled the cards with the ease and fluid motion of an expert, all the while keeping her eyes trained on David and her smile wide. "Do me one last favor. Take the card from the top of the deck."

David reached out cautiously and turned over the top card. It was the seven of clubs.

Dorinda soaked up the look of surprise on David's face. "I do card tricks," she nodded. "And more advanced than that. I can cut the deck so that one half is all black cards and one half is all reds. Without even looking."

"Wow," said David.

Dorinda signaled the waiter that they were ready to order. "You probably didn't know I could do that. Kellyn thinks it's lame, so I mostly do it when I visit my grandparents. I cook, too. And I don't just mean I know how to switch on the food processor. My specialty is chorizo, ricotta, and soft egg ravioli with Parma ham. Giada De Laurentiis is like an icon to me. I'm seriously thinking about going to culinary school. That's something else you probably didn't know about me. Something else that was dismissed as lame by certain parties. But I thought you should be aware." Dorinda gazed at David with an unsettling intensity. "So you had the proper information to make your choice. So you weren't pressured by the first person who came along and seemed like she was right for you but totally wasn't."

The waiter approached David and Dorinda. He was about to take their order when Kellyn shoved him aside so roughly that he staggered backward, knocking over the water jug on the next table.

Kellyn's face was red. She was breathing hard. She looked like she'd been running. She looked like she could barely contain her fury. Dorinda didn't even register her former best friend's sudden appearance at the table. Neither did she acknowledge the apologetic, "Um . . . she made me tell her where you were," from the front of the restaurant.

Dorinda addressed her attention to her deck of cards.

Kellyn stared furiously at the confused David. "How could you be so dumb? She sent us both fake texts. I was smart enough to know that you'd never, *ever* choose a night hanging out with your friends over spending time with me. But how could you ever in a million years think that I'd want to be seen at *the Cheesecake Factory*?" Kellyn said this loud enough to attract the attention of the staff and patrons of the restaurant, most of whom looked her way with open disapproval.

Dorinda glanced up from her cards and shook her head sadly at Kellyn. "There's nothing wrong with the Cheesecake Factory. It's a high-volume chain that never sacrifices the quality." Smiling at David, Dorinda gestured to Kellyn and said, "She's such a snob. It's an ugly trait. Again, just keeping you informed."

"You crossed the line," snarled Kellyn to Dorinda.

"I redrew the line," replied a calm Dorinda. "I made it fair."

Kellyn was about to argue. Instead, she inhaled and seemed to visibly calm. She snapped a finger at the waiter she'd pushed and said, "Another chair."

Two minutes later, David found himself sitting across a table from Kellyn and Dorinda, both of whom were eying him closely.

"Looks like someone's got a big choice to make," said Kellyn.

"Let's hope they've got all the information," said Dorinda, manipulating her pack of cards so that the queen of hearts poked her head above the rest.

"Lame," muttered Kellyn.

"You're lame," retorted Dorinda.

"I've got to go to the bathroom," squeaked David, pushing his chair back and fleeing the table.

TWENTY-TWO
Cookies for Geeks

Spending time around people whose lives she considered pathetic was always therapeutic for Pixie. Which is why she set out to salvage her tragic Saturday night by paying a surprise visit to the eighth floor of Furmanovsky Industries. In Pixie's experience *no one* was more socially unskilled and deprived of any form of attention than the engineers, innovators, prodigies, and geniuses who worked in her father's Research & Development office. They had no lives. They had no friends. They had no fashion sense. All they had was their huge misshapen throbbing brains. Brains, her father assured her, that were one day going to make Furmanovsky Industries the corporation that changed the way the world worked.

Pixie recalled her father predicting his company would make

billions when it started mass-producing invisible cars and instant clone sprays. But what really excited her about the geeks on the eighth floor was that she could easily persuade them to give her free stuff. That's how she got the *pixie*Phone. "It's not really ready," they'd stammered. "It needs a few more modifications and another round of testing." To which Pixie had smiled and responded with an earsplitting, "I WANT IT NOW!"

Pixie stopped outside the door leading toward Research & Development. She widened her eyes and allowed the security system to take a retinal scan. Her identity confirmed, she skipped through the doors as they slid open and made her way into the heart of R&D.

The scientists who worked in the department didn't know if it was Saturday night or Christmas Eve. Their focus was completely on their work, and nothing could distract them. *Almost* nothing.

"Hello, nerds!" trilled Pixie cheerfully.

Eyes started blinking rapidly. Brows grew moist. The boss's daughter's unexpected visits always threw the scientists into panics.

"Look," she said, holding up a basket, "I brought cookies!" So saying, she began tossing treats to the innovators. "Snickerdoodle!" she announced, throwing a cookie to a nearby physicist. "Rice Krispie Treat!" she yelled, lobbing a confection at a famed robotics engineer. "And I *know* somebody around here just *looooves* their vanilla shortbread," she cooed in a teasing voice. "Come and get it, Raj!"

The mathematical genius had looked as petrified as his colleagues at Pixie's sudden, shock appearance. But now that she was in the R&D lab, she seemed so sweet and small and unthreat-ening. And the vanilla shortbread she was holding just slightly above his upturned mouth seemed so tempting. Pixie dropped the cookie into Raj's mouth, watched him devour it, and smiled at the way his eyes widened in sugary pleasure. Then she sat down beside him, took his hand in hers, beamed up at him with huge wide innocent eyes, and asked, "So, Raj, what have you got for me?"

Raj was reluctant. The R&D department was involved in supersecret work. They were involved with the army. With the FBI. With the CIA. With the CIZ: the extra-double-covert shadow organization that no one was entirely sure even existed. But Pixie *was* the boss's daughter, and she had a combination of charm and intimidation that tended to get her whatever she desired. (Plus, Raj's nutritionist had expressly warned him to stay away from vanilla shortbread because it made him *nuts*.) So Raj gave Pixie a Saturday-night guided tour of the latest inno-vations the combined brains of the R&D department had been working on.

He showed her the iPill, an iPod in pill form with 60 GB of tunes available in one swallow; the Butter into Plastic machine, a vast furnacelike device that turned butter into plastic and, so far, had no other uses; and the Pet Nightmare Toon Player, a screen that captured the bad dreams of animals and replayed them in hilarious animated form. These inventions were of zero inter-est to Pixie. What she wanted—although she would never have admitted this to herself—was something that would produce a reaction like the *pixie*Phone had from Alison. Something that would make Alison die with envy. Something that would make Alison want to be her friend again.

But Raj hadn't been able to produce anything so special. Pixie was resigned to writing off her trip to the nerd factory as a waste of time when she caught sight of something glinting enticingly from an unattended computer screen.

"What's *that?*" she said. Without waiting for an answer, Pixie rushed over to the screen.

Raj followed nervously. His face fell when he saw Pixie drooling over a high-resolution picture of a dress. Not just any dress. This one was made from a sort of gold silk that seemed to shimmer as if was made from millions of tiny lights. It was the most beautiful thing she'd ever seen.

Pixie beamed up at Raj. "Yes, please," she said.

Raj closed his eyes for a second. He wished he was dealing with quadratic residues and not some frightening undeniable little girl whose pupils were blasting *Surrender To My Charisma* commands into his brain. He wished he hadn't eaten so much vanilla shortbread. He went through the motions of putting up a fight.

"That . . . uh. . . particular item . . . is . . . uh . . . earmarked for special use in the field of . . . uh . . . covert intelligence . . . It's still in the testing stage, but when it's perfected, it's intended for the use of trained professionals." *There*, he thought, *I put my foot down. Boss's daughter or not. She can't have the gold dress.*

Pixie let her chin sink into her palms. She nodded understandingly at Raj, gave a cute little shrug, and then screamed, "I WANT IT NOW!"

TWENTY-THREE

Bizarre Love Triangle

$\mathcal{D}avid$ *didn't use* the bathroom at the Cheesecake Factory. Instead, he hurried out of the family-fun restaurant, jumped into the nearest cab, and made his way to the door of the one person who could help him make sense of his sudden and entirely unexpected romantic predicament.

Designated Dean told him a lengthy story about a club in Santa Monica that had a giant cereal bowl where girls wrestled in gallons of milk and attempted to beat each other senseless with huge plastic spoons. David listened intently and thanked Designated Dean for taking the time to talk to him. Then he made his way to the door of the only other person who might be able to help him make sense of his sudden and entirely unexpected romantic entanglement.

"Wowza!" said Alison after David had told her about his date with Kellyn and Dorinda.

"Yup," said David, sitting by the window of Alison's bedroom, looking out at her pool.

Turning to face her, he rattled out a quick, despairing, "So what should I do? Should I do anything? Should I not do anything? What would you do?"

Alison sat on the edge of her bed. She recognized how much it had taken for him to approach her for advice. They had been best friends at the dawn of Alison's transformation into Hottie, but David was not by nature a confider. And then he'd developed a painful crush on her. Even though they'd got beyond that weirdness, their relationship had not reverted to what it had once been. Over the past few months, it had seemed like they were only technically friends because they had a mutual friend in common. And that mutual friend was a superhero. But now she had the opportunity to get her best friend back. Alison looked at the confused but hopeful expression on David's face and realized what she said next held the key to reestablishing their relationship.

She walked over to David and sat down on a bamboo chair a few feet from the window. Holding his gaze, she said, "You know how you liked me and that didn't happen? Do you think maybe you're hanging out with them 'cuz they're like the closest thing you can get to me?"

David didn't say a word. He walked quickly away from the window and headed for the door. Alison cursed inwardly. That was *totally* the wrong thing to say. It *was* something she'd wondered deep down, but as soon as she saw David's reaction, she knew that it was a *thought*, it wasn't a *say*.

"Sorrysorrysorrysorry. Wait. Stop. Come back!" Alison threw herself in front of the bedroom door, kicking it shut behind her. David was inches away. He looked angrier and more hurt than she'd ever seen him.

"You're a jerk," he finally muttered.

She nodded in agreement. "I am a jerk."

"That's what you think?" he asked, still annoyed. "That I'm still hung up on you?"

Alison tried to lead David back into the room. "I was kidding. I was completely kidding. I wasn't actually kidding at all. I was talking without thinking. I was being the Alison-thinks-the-world-revolves-around-her idiot that Kellyn and Dorinda think I am."

She sat down on her bed. David stood in the middle of the room, hands shoved deep into his pockets, eyes everywhere but Alison's face.

You get a do over. Do it right this time, she told herself. "So I've been thinking about this problem of yours," she said, as if they'd just started talking. "And you know what's funny? I myself have been in the exact same situation. I know it's hard to believe, but there was once a time, many years ago, when I was still young and had all my senses, that two people of the boy persuasion both thought they liked me."

"Hard to believe," muttered David.

"I know, right?" Alison nodded. "They were both amazing, and I hated to have to hurt either one of them. But you have to follow your heart—"

"Hang on, I never heard that before," interrupted David

sarcastically. "Did you just make that up? What was it again, something about following your heart?"

Alison carried on, unperturbed. "Yeah, I'm kind of a genius. Why do you think they both liked me?" Turning serious, she said, "I know how you feel. I know what you're going through. It's awful to feel like you're responsible for someone else's feelings. To know that you could just crush them if you say or do the wrong thing. But you've got to do what's going to make you happy—that's another one I just made up, straight off the top of my head."

David's anger at Alison had faded. He couldn't fight his smile.

Alison held out a hand and pulled David over to the bed. He sat down next to her. "The difference in our situations is, I had to choose between two fantastic guys, and you're caught in the middle of two insane nutballs. But, if you're lucky like I was lucky, you'll still end up with an incredible friend."

David said nothing for a moment. Then he nodded at her. "Thanks," he mumbled, and headed for the door.

"Was I any help?" Alison called after him.

David waggled his hand in a so-so gesture.

"Was I at least more help than Designated Dean?"

Just before he left the bedroom, David turned around and grinned at Alison. As he headed downstairs, she lay back on her bed and breathed a sigh of relief. She had her best friend back.

Outside Alison's house, David stood in the cold of the Brentwood night and pulled out his phone. He was about to call Designated Dean to come pick him up. Then he decided to make a different call. He listened as the phone rang and then said, "The Cheesecake Factory is a really good affordable restaurant, and we're gonna go back there, and you're gonna say sorry to the waiter you shoved . . ."

TWENTY-FOUR
Electric Butterfly

The nerds from R&D were freaking out.

"Raj!" they whined. "Why did you let her try on the dress?"

"Raj!" they howled. "It's a prototype! It's not ready. The tests haven't been completed!"

"Raj!" they wept. "There should be a member of staff on hand in case something goes wrong."

Raj took note of his colleagues' complaints. But the matter was out of his hands. Pixie had pulled out her *pixie*Phone and begun to send a text to the fourth floor of Furmanovsky Industries. The floor where Pixie's father's private-security force trained. The floor where screams of pain and gunshots were clearly audible through solid steel walls. Pixie let her finger hover over the buttons. That hovering motion was enough to convince Raj to gather his workmates and lead them out of the building for the first coffee break they'd taken in four and a half years.

Alone in the Prototype Testing Room, Pixie looked at her reflection in the mirror that stretched out the length of an entire wall.

"I look like a different girl," she said.

Back in her Malibu home, Pixie had a special room that was bursting with her enormous collection of clothes, but nothing in that room had ever, even for a second, made her feel the way she did when she looked at herself in the gold dress.

She pulled the hood of the dress over her head and gasped at the way it cast shadows over her face. "I look so mysterious," she said, amazed. She gazed in awe at the tiny lights that traveled up and down the dress. She opened her arms wide and the gold silk fell like bat wings. The material gathered tightly around her wrists and continued to coil in gold tendrils up to her fingertips.

Keeping her arms extended, she began to whirl around. Gasping at the way the dress threw sparks and flashes of gold light around the room, she spun faster. "I feel like a disco ball!" She laughed out loud. Pixie kept laughing. Her suckfest of a Saturday night had culminated in an unbelievably happy ending. She closed her eyes and continued spinning. *I've never felt like this*, she thought. *I don't care what anyone thinks of me. I don't care what my daddy thinks. I don't care if anyone likes me or not. As long as I'm wearing this dress, I feel like I'm walking on air.*

And then Pixie opened her eyes and saw that she was, in fact, walking on air. To be exact, she was floating six feet above the ground. She stopped spinning and started screaming. In the midst of her mounting hysteria, Pixie didn't notice the white bolts of electricity that had begun to crackle around the gold tendrils.

"Help!" she screamed. "Get me down!"

The more she hurled her arms around, the more violently the electricity sparked around the tendrils. Finally, Pixie became aware of the pulsing sensation playing around her fingers. She stopped screaming and concentrated on the electrical activity occurring around her fingers. Pixie watched, fascinated, as the volts traveled around the gold tendrils. She forgot she'd been abandoned by her father and her supposed new best friend. Pixie began to slowly descend so that she could get a good look at herself in the Testing Room Mirror.

Coming to a halt, twelve inches off the ground, Pixie stared at her reflection. She loved that she could defy gravity. She loved the way her fingers crackled and sparked. The only thing she didn't like was how cute and innocent she looked. Her whole life, she'd worked hard to maintain that sweet exterior. So that people would like her. Not because she was Ludovic Furmanovsky's daughter. But because she was a nice, kind, caring girl. And she'd been disappointed. The more she tried to make friends, the more disappointed she became. Everyone let her down. Her mother was dead. Her father was never home. The *Jen* editors were unreliable. Alison couldn't wait to get away from her. *So what?* she found herself thinking. *Why waste my time with friends when I've got* power?

Pixie bared her teeth as she smiled at her floating reflection. "I look like a little angel," she murmured to her mirror image. "But I'm not a little angel anymore." With that, she reached out a hand and sent a blast of electricity into the mirror. Shards of glass exploded across the Prototype Testing Room. Pixie rose into the air and looked down at the carnage below with a big grin.

"Raj, we don't hear any sound from in there," whimpered the R&D staff as they gathered fearfully outside the Testing Room.

"Raj, what if her father set this whole thing up to test us?" They shuddered.

"Raj, go in and see if she's okay," they demanded.

"Why do I have to do it?" asked Raj.

"You let her try on the dress," they chorused.

Nodding glumly, Raj tapped gently on the Testing Room door. "Miss Furmanovsky? Everything okay in there?"

No response.

Raj tapped a little louder. "Miss Furmanovsky?"

Not a sound.

Raj felt his heart begin to pound. The prototype. The boss's daughter. The coffee break. This might have been a bad combination. Raj hammered his fists on the door. "I'm coming in! Don't worry! I'm a noted mathematician!" Just as the adrenaline had ignited Raj into an action hero, the Prototype Testing Room's door opened.

Pixie strolled out, still clad in the gold dress. She smiled at Raj and waved to the rest of the R&D department, who were cowering further down the corridor.

The scientists stared at her in amazement. Pixie soaked up their awe, enjoying the expressions on their faces.

Finally, she simply said, "I know," and walked past them toward the elevators.

The R&D department turned to Raj. "Do something," they insisted.

Raj swallowed his fear and hurried after Pixie. "Can we have the dress back? As I mentioned, it's the only one of its kind. It's intended for use in the field of international espionage . . ."

Pixie turned to Raj and reached out a finger. The second she touched his hand, a bolt of electricity caused him to shudder in shock. Delighting in his reaction, Pixie put a finger to her lips. "Sssh," she whispered. "Not a word to anyone. Or I'll come back and see you again. And you *really* wouldn't want that." Pixie gave Raj a wink and then walked away.

The mathematician stared after her. He was still trembling. But it wasn't *entirely* because of the shock. He couldn't get over the expression on her face. Her *eyes*. They were still huge. They were still impossible to ignore. But they weren't charming anymore. They were *evil*.

TWENTY-FIVE

Blondes and Brazilians

15 . . . 16 . . . 17 . . .

As the elevator headed toward the twenty-third floor, Alison thought about how she was going to handle The Pixie Situation. So far she'd handled it by totally bailing on her dream job. She'd called in sick for the past few afternoons. She'd contemplated simply not going back to *Jen*. But that was a quitter's way out. And Alison wasn't a quitter . . .

18 . . . 19 . . . 20 . . .

This was how she was going to approach Pixie. She'd thank her profusely for mentoring her. But, Alison would say, she didn't think she'd be getting everything she could from the intern experience if she didn't give working in all the other departments a chance. Which meant stepping out from under Pixie's wing.

21 . . . 22 . . . 23

Alison began to wonder if she was doing the right thing. Stepping out from under Pixie's wing meant no more special treatment. She would be distancing herself from a powerful friend and deliberately asking to be seen as just another intern. Which meant that she could hang out with the other interns and gossip with them about how *weird* Pixie was.

The elevator doors opened on the twenty-third floor. The wheelchair-bound Elspeth rolled in, her eyes red and puffy. A cardboard box with all her workplace belongings spilling over the top sat in her lap. "Don't go in there," she warned, her voice shaky.

Alison was surprised by the expression on Elspeth's face. She wasn't just crying, she was *terrified*.

"What's happened?"

The photographer gazed up at Alison. "It's Pixie," she whispered. "She's . . . she . . . you'll see for yourself." With that, Elspeth reached out and pressed the ground-floor button.

Alison jumped out of the elevator. As the doors closed, she could see the photographer burst into a fresh batch of tears. Even before Alison turned around and walked into the reception area, she could *feel* the heavy sense of dread that suddenly hung over the *Jen* office. The first change she noticed was behind the reception desk.

Where once Cutesy Woo sat looking fragrant and fragile, there was now a six-foot blonde who ignored the shrill chorus of ringing phones in favor of applying a fresh coat of lip gloss. Alison made her way to Pixie's Palace to extricate herself from her mood-swinging editor's grasp. Two big burly black-clad men stood on either side of the door. One of them had a face like a bowling ball. The other had an eye-catching kelly green lightning-bolt-shaped Mohawk growing in the center of his otherwise shorn skull. As Alison got closer, they inched their way together, barring her way.

"Hi," she said. "Can I go in? Or is Pixie in a meeting?"

Bowling Ball Face pulled out a BlackBerry. He scrolled down the screen until he found Alison's picture and accompanying information. "Intern," he croaked.

"You live in the intern room," growled Green Lightning Bolt Head. "Why aren't you there?"

Alison felt a burning sensation in her fingertips. "Because I want to talk to my friend," she said, trying to keep a lid on her temper.

Bowling Ball Face scowled at her. "You're walking away from here or I'm dragging you. Either way, you don't get through this door."

Alison stared at the two big men. Then she reached into her bag and pulled out a black eyebrow pencil. She tossed it to Bowling Ball Face. "In case you want to draw them back in. After I've burned them off."

The two guys exchanged looks. They walked toward Alison, aggression evident in their every movement. Alison cracked her knuckles. She was ready to burn these guys down to cinders.

Just before the flames flew from her fingers, Waris, the gap-toothed Somali, came charging up. She placed herself firmly between the two opposing parties. "She doesn't know," the girl explained to the angry guys.

"Know what?" demanded Alison.

Instead of explaining, Waris grabbed Alison by the hand and dragged her away from the white door. Alison was about to pull her hand free and repeat, "Know what?" But as her rescuer dragged her away from the reception area, Alison started to become aware of more changes to the fun, friendly *Jen*-osphere. A willowy blonde with plumped-up lips teetered out of the entertainment department. An even taller, even skinnier Brazilian girl, who looked like she'd just rolled out of bed, wandered out of the beauty department. More impossibly tall, impossibly gorgeous girls, all blonde and/or Brazilian, seemed to melt out of all the other departments.

Alison stared at them in increasing confusion. None of them paid the slightest bit of attention to her. Waris pulled Alison inside the intern room. The door closed behind her. Alison turned to see her friends from the beach—Amandine, the shovel-jawed entertainment editor, and all the other *Jen* employees that Pixie had praised as "my pick of the best." They looked scared and sad and beaten down.

"Why are you in the intern room when you're editors?" asked Alison, who had an inkling she wouldn't like the answer.

"We were demoted," mumbled Amandine.

"She took our jobs away," said Waris. "She hired all those tall blondes and Brazilians."

"She said we could stay on as interns or we could leave," continued Amandine. "But we'd never get jobs anywhere else."

Alison looked around the intern room. She saw the former managing editor counting buttons and putting them in boxes.

"And Pixie just sprang this on you? Without a word?" Alison demanded.

The ex-editors hung their heads. Before they could reply, the intern-room door flew open. Bowling Ball Face and Green Lightning Bolt Head walked in. They took up positions on either side of the door.

"Oh My God," gasped Alison, catching sight of the next person to walk through the door. "*Pixie?*"

"Great observational ability, Alison," replied an irritated voice. "No one's pulling the wool over your eyes. The stupid, maybe. But not the wool."

Alison stared at the girl who'd just insulted her. The crimson lips. The jet black bob cut sharp enough to draw blood. The severe black business suit. The six-inch stilettos. The icy, unsmiling expression. It was Pixie. But it *wasn't* the Pixie Alison knew.

Pixie gave Alison a brief, contemptuous eye roll. Then she addressed the residents of the intern room. "You know what I'm looking at?" she asked the group of trembling ex-editors. "I'm looking at the old *Jen*. And the old *Jen* was for losers. The old *Jen* was the fat girl's friend." This said with a cold stare straight at Amandine. "This is the new *Jen*. The new *Jen* is about three things: famous, rich, and skinny. That's all I want to see in our photos. That's all I want to read about in our features. That's all I want to see when I walk down the corridors. Obviously, that's not what I see in front of me."

"Is this something to do with what happened on Saturday night?" Alison piped up.

Pixie stared daggers at Alison, who once again vowed to learn the difference between a thought and a say.

"*Never* address me personally," Pixie stormed. "This is what

I'm talking about. None of you fit the new *Jen* brand. I ought to have you all thrown out in the street."

At this, Pixie's security guards began to rub their hands in gleeful anticipation.

"But I'm giving you one last chance. If you make yourselves indispensable to the new editors, if you do whatever they say, and if they deliver positive reports, maybe I'll let you stay on. If not . . ." Pixie made a familiar dismissive gesture. "Out with the garbage."

Having delivered her scary pronouncement, Pixie struck further terror into the heart of her former inner circle by snapping her fingers. At her snap, the squadron of impossibly blonde, impossibly tall, impossibly Brazilian editors marched into the intern room. The blondes and Brazilians surveyed the interns as if they were at the dog pound, appraising stray puppies. Stray puppies they planned to terrorize and abuse.

One by one, the former editors were hauled away to their new fates. All except Alison, who was left standing by herself.

"Awww," Pixie pretend-pouted. "Looks like no one wants little Alison."

Alison couldn't stop staring at the change in Pixie. It wasn't just the razor blade hair. It wasn't just the sky-high heels or the forbidding black suit. Her big eyes—the ones that previously implored, *Please like me*—now shone with superiority. There was something about her that seemed . . . *evil*.

"What's going on, Pixie?" asked Alison, trying to find a trace of the girl who was recently so eager to be her friend. "Who are all these blondes and Brazilians?"

"They're the heart and soul of *Jen*," Pixie replied in mocking, hushed tones. "They're the face I want the world to see, and—I don't know if you noticed—it's not a *fat* face."

"And the stupid-looking guys guarding your door?"

"The finest recruits from my daddy's private-security firm."

Alison shook her head in confusion. "To protect you from what?"

Pixie smoothed out her perfect, shiny bob. "Maybe they're to protect *you* . . ." She let the sentence hang.

She's trying to intimidate me, thought Alison. *And it's working*! Making an effort to appear unruffled, Alison went on. "I thought we were all part of the same family."

"We are," smirked Pixie. "It's just that some of us are the ugly, slow, embarrassing members of the family, who get locked in the basement out of sight."

Pixie's amusement at her own arrogance infuriated Alison. "I thought there was no difference between you and the readers," she said, the accusation evident in her voice.

"Of course, there's a difference," snapped Pixie. "I'm brilliant and accomplished and mature and responsible, and I'm worth billions. I want them to be sick with envy when they see me."

Alison couldn't contain her distress. "You hypocritic. You sold out everything you said you believed in."

Pixie's eyes darkened. She took a step toward Alison, all the while rubbing her thumbs and forefingers together. "Don't get on my bad side, Alison," she said in a low warning voice. "Make me mad, and the interns will be shoveling bits of you into buckets."

Alison stared at Pixie. Then she noticed the girl's fingers. She felt a sudden chill of apprehension. The appearance in the intern room of a tiny birdlike figure wrapped in a black business suit and wearing six-inch heels diffused the tension.

"Ah." Pixie smiled. "Here's your new owner. Serve her well, and maybe you'll get to hang around a little longer."

Alison stared at the new girl in the room. She had the same black bob. The same sneer. It wasn't until the smell of jasmine filled her nostrils that she recognized her new boss.

"Don't just stand there," commanded Cutesy Woo. "I need you to degum my shoes."

"What?" asked Alison.

Pixie's grin lit up the room. "The new managing editor requires that you degum her shoes. So snap to it, intern!"

TWENTY-SIX

Crush

$\mathcal{A}$*lison couldn't believe* she was sitting on the floor of Cutesy Woo's spacious office using her keys to scrape calcified chewing gum off the sole of her new boss's cream Balenciaga booties.

"Finished?" chirped Cutesy Woo.

Alison held up the gum-free shoes as proof.

Cutesy scowled, picked up a remote, and aimed it at the far wall of the office, which was filled with framed *Jen* covers. One cover seemed to split in two. The sections of a false wall separated, revealing twelve backlit rows of shoes.

"No, you haven't," peeped Cutesy Woo.

As Alison buckled down to do her demeaning task, she had no idea her boyfriend was riding the elevator up to *Jen*.

T wondered if Alison would be mad that he was springing a surprise visit on her. He thought not. Her hilarious stories about life at the teen magazine had intrigued him. Showing an interest in *her* interests was a good way to finally dispel any lingering resentment that might have remained from his ill-conceived accusation of immaturity.

When T stepped out on the twenty-third floor, he saw the amazing bedazzled reception area that Alison had described. He saw the animated front covers lining the walls. But he didn't see any signs of humanity. All the blondes and Brazilians were taking bathroom breaks, as they did every twenty minutes since the moment they'd been hired.

Pixie's security guards had been dispatched to the city's newsstands and given the important task of hiding all the *Pink Sugar* covers behind the new issues of *Jen*. The former editors had all been given to-do lists so humiliating they only wished they could be de-gumming shoes.

T waited in the reception area for a moment. He started to call Alison but decided that would defeat the purpose of the surprise visit. So he made his way into the heart of the magazine. The doors he passed were locked. The muffled sounds on the other side sounded like weeping. Then he approached the door with the glittery name PIXIE'S PALACE. T smiled. This was where Alison said she spent much of her *Jen* time. He knocked on the door.

"Come," barked a voice.

T wasn't sure who he was about to encounter, but something made him stand a little straighter, push his shoulders back, and draw himself up to his full height just before he pushed the office door open. Then he walked into Pixie's office.

"Hi, I was looking for Alison. Alison Cole?"

"Well, as you can see, she's not here, so . . ." Pixie glanced up from her laptop to dismiss the intruder. Then she saw T standing in the doorway, and the rest of her sentence died in her mouth.

"I'm T. Well, Tommy, actually. But people call me T. I'm friends with Alison. She wasn't expecting me. So if this is a bad time, maybe you could tell her I was here and . . ."

"Oh My Gosh," gasped Pixie, jumping out of her throne and leaping over the cushions in her hurry to get to T. The superior sneer was entirely absent from her face. She was suddenly all sweetness and smiles. "This is an *awesome* time. It's so amazing to see you. Allywally's talked *so* much about you. Sit down, make yourself at home, she'll be back in a minute. God, she'll be *so* surprised to see you . . ."

Alison had never discussed T with Pixie. But she had told T, on more than one occasion, that Pixie was a warm, caring, generous person. T found this to be an understatement. Pixie was blasting him with her full allocation of charm, breathless enthusiasm, and boundless interest.

And, just as Alison once had, T found himself thinking, *She's so nice.*

Alison had had enough. There was something stuck to the bottom of Cutesy Woo's Miu Miu peep-toe Mary Janes, and it didn't look or smell like Doublemint. Alison tossed the shoes aside, jumped to her feet, and headed out the office door.

"Get back to work!" demanded Cutesy Woo. But Alison wasn't interested in following barely audible orders. She was more interested in confronting Pixie.

★ ★ ★

T was inputting his information into the *pixie*Phone when Alison threw open the palace door. "We need to talk!" she said.

"Allywally!" squealed Pixie happily.

"Pixie Stix," murmured Alison, taking in the sight of T lying on the comfy cushions. Shoes off. A few empty Vitaminwater bottles. In-N-Out Burger wrappers. *Very cozy.*

T waved at Alison and brandished the one-of-a kind phone. "Isn't this *amazing?*"

"Amazing," Alison echoed. She had completely forgotten her plans to confront Pixie.

"I told him he can have it once the next-next-next . . ."

Alison finished the sentence. "Next-next generation comes out. I remember."

"Where have you *been?*" implored Pixie. "We've missed you so much, haven't we, T-Bird?"

T-Bird. Alison aimed a pointed smile at T, hoping that he knew her well enough to be able to understand that her smile wasn't really a smile at all. It was a warning to exercise extreme caution. T smiled back at her, completely unaware of what the expression on her face was actually saying.

Pixie reached out and squeezed T's forearm. "Where have you been keeping this guy? We need him around all the time. I love all my *Jen* girls, but it's so helpful to have a little male input now and again." At the exact same moment Pixie was flirting shamelessly with T, she moved her head ever so slightly and *winked* at Alison. And Alison understood that Pixie's wink wasn't really a wink at all. It was a declaration of war from a vast and wealthy continent to a small, defenseless island.

T pointed to the *pixie*Phone. "You know the number. Call me anytime."

Pixie touched a key. A 3-D hologram of T's smiling face suddenly floated above the phone. Pixie smiled happily both at the real guy and the image she'd captured. She squeezed his forearm one more time.

Uh-oh, thought Alison.

TWENTY-SEVEN

I Want You to Want Me

"So what did you think of Pixie?" asked Alison casually as T drove her back to Brentwood.

"Nice," replied T, equally casually.

"She's *really* cute, isn't she?"

T had an idea where Alison's line of inquiry was headed. He kept his eyes on the road and his voice even and noncommittal. "She's all right."

"She liked you. A lot."

Once again, T stared straight ahead. "Why wouldn't she?" He smiled. "I'm likable."

Alison said nothing for a moment. Then she asked, "She didn't seem kinda *weird* to you?"

"Weird how?"

"I don't know." Alison shrugged. "Just weird. Like you'd be talking to her, and she suddenly turned into another person."

T grinned. "What? Like she has a *secret identity*?"

"Forget it." Alison ended her interrogation and stared out of the window for the rest of the journey. Before she got out of the car, she pushed a folded-up piece of paper into his jacket pocket.

"What's that?" he said.

"It's nothing," she replied. "Forget about it. It's something I don't want to talk about now because it'll sound like I'm crazy and *immature*, and I don't want to fight. But one day I might remind you that it's there and ask you to open it."

"You're an open book." T grinned. "No secrets. Nothing mysterious."

Alison gave him a rueful smile and headed indoors.

T turned the Chevy Impala around and began the drive back to his home in the architecturally pleasing area of Los Feliz. A moment later, his phone rang. The word *Pixie* appeared on the screen. T's eyebrows rose. *Speak of the devil.* He picked up.

"Hi, T? It's Pixie Furmanovsky. From *Jen* magazine?"

"I remember," said T.

"I've been thinking. That thing I was saying about needing male input in the magazine? We absolutely need a column that gives our readers the male perspective. If there's one thing I hear more than anything from them, it's 'What's going on in boys' heads?' Maybe that's what the column could be called: What's Going On In Boys' Heads?"

T waited for a break in Pixie's excited outpouring. "Good idea," he said.

"So, do you wanna do it?" she asked.

T wasn't sure what she was asking so he stayed silent.

"*The column!*" she yelped. "Do you wanna write it?"

"Me?" T found himself asking.

"Why not you?" she said. "You're a boy. There's stuff going on in your head. My readers want to know what it is. Look, you don't have to commit to anything—I know that's something *every* guy likes to hear—just give it some thought. If you want, we can get together and talk about it some more. Gotta go. Hit me back whenever. Bye."

And then she was gone and T's head was full of conflicting thoughts. *I really want to do this* was T's first thought. *She's not weird at all* was his second thought. *She's totally smart and all business* was his third thought. *I should probably tell Alison about this* was his fourth thought. *But if I tell her, she'll be all freaked out, and she'll ask me a million questions* was his fifth thought.

T drove in silence for a moment. The thought of Alison's endless passive-aggressive questioning was not something he was looking forward to. *But I really want to do this* was his final thought.

The following afternoon, while Alison was in the fashion closet running a lint remover over mountainous piles of fuzzy dresses, T found himself sitting poolside with Pixie under an umbrella-shaded table at the Cabana Club Café in the ancient and revered Beverly Hills Hotel. T didn't know whether he was more wowed by the sumptuous surroundings, the acres of toned, tanned bikini-clad movie-star bodies on display, or the mature, experienced way Pixie conducted herself. Over the duration of their forty-five-minute meeting, she had extracted a year's worth of column ideas from him and instilled in him the confidence that he could attract and hold on to the interest of the *Jen* readership. T didn't know what impressed him most: that Pixie was so smart and businesslike or the way she was able to maintain her credibility as a teen tycoon, while simultaneously shrieking with giddy, girlish delight when the waiter delivered a towering heap of ice-cream sundae to the table.

It took T thirty minutes to drive back from the Beverly Hills Hotel to Los Feliz. During that time, he continued to think about Pixie and how amazing and un-neurotic and together she was. How she was so full of empathy. How she had no secrets. While he continued the drive home, a brand-new Porsche 911 was being gift wrapped and delivered to the Hull home. When T returned to Los Feliz, he got out of his Chevy Impala and whistled appreciatively at the gleaming new vehicle. T's father was standing out in the street staring at the car. As his son approached, T-Dad detached an envelope from the door of the Porsche. The letter *T* was written on the front of the envelope. Inside were the car keys.

Two mornings later, T wandered down to the kitchen to fix a quick breakfast, only to find a man already busy making toast and squeezing oranges. A man wearing Barneys leather loafers and a Breitling watch.

"Please join the others," requested the man. "Breakfast will be served shortly."

T was so surprised he couldn't manage more than a grunt and an obedient nod. Then he walked into the dining room, where his father, Swedish stepmother, Birgit, and younger brother, Drew, sat around the table. They all had tight polite smiles on their faces. They all aimed inquisitive stares in his direction. The reason for the smiles and the stares was the other occupant at the table: a girl with a heart-shaped face and a jet black bob.

"Good morning, sleepyhead," she said, bouncing up to hug him.

I should probably tell Alison about this, thought T as he drove Pixie to *Jen* in the shiny new Porsche, which, she assured him, her Daddy's dealership loaned out to prospective clients for extended test-drives all the time. *But she might misunderstand. Or get mad. And there's nothing to get mad about. Pixie's just really friendly. And, anyway, it's business. The column.*

"Hey," said Pixie as she was about to slide out of the Porsche. "You a Lakers fan?"

"You might say that," T said, nodding.

"Only 'might?'" taunted Pixie. "My Daddy's got a courtside season pass. I was gonna ask you if you wanted to go to a game. But if it's only 'might' . . ."

"It's not 'might,'" relented T. "It's *please*. Anytime."

I should probably tell Alison about this, thought T, sitting in English class the following morning. Pixie had sent him *another* photo of herself in a cute Laker Girl cheerleader uniform. He was starting to feel uncomfortable, as if she was under the impression they were *more* than friends. But then he thought, *Alison doesn't need to know about this. Pixie's just got a quirky sense of humor. It's nothing I need to feel guilty about. And, anyway, it's business. The column.*

And then, during math, the principal's assistant had interrupted the class and gestured to T to follow her. A ripple of concern filled the room. The principal's assistant only showed up when there was bad news to impart.

"What's happened?" T asked the assistant.

"I'll let your sister explain," she replied.

T was about to say, "I don't have a sister," when he saw Pixie waiting by the assistant's desk. She ran up and threw her arms around him.

"It's so awful about Grandma," she sobbed. "But at least we get to say goodbye." And then she grabbed T's arm and pulled him down the corridor, barely able to stifle her laughter.

"What are you *doing*?" T tried to keep his voice calm, but he was aghast. Fearing that someone might see him with Pixie, he pushed her into a supply closet.

"You can't just show up like this," he hissed.

"I can do anything I want," she replied, upturning a box of pencils. "And right now, I want to have fun. So stop being such a boring schoolboy and let's go do something."

"Pixie, you need to leave right now."

She gave him an irritated stare. Then she said, "I'll scream. I'll scream really loud, and I'll tell everyone that you dragged me in here. Which is true."

T looked into her eyes. She displayed no evidence of a quirky sense of humor. She was dead serious.

"Okay," he said soothingly, as if to an angry child. "What do you want to do?"

She was beaming again. "Everything," she squealed.

Pixie decided she wanted to go bowling. A quick call to her daddy and the Lucky Strike lanes in Hollywood opened early just for her and T. Pixie wanted to shop at the Beverly Center. A quick call and the mall was temporarily closed to every customer but her and T. Pixie decided she wanted to see a movie at the plush ArcLight Cinema on Sunset Boulevard. A quick call and the cinema was reserved solely for her and T. During the movie, she put her head on his shoulder and whispered, "I want it to be like this, always."

T said nothing. He felt her breath get closer to his ear. He squirmed as she said, "I'd really like it if you came to my sweet sixteen."

After the movie, they walked down to the ArcLight parking garage. Pixie reached for T's hand.

I've got to stop this now, he decided. "This has been fun and you're great, and I can't wait to get to work on the column, but I've got to get back to school and make up what I missed today. Thank your father for the test-drive."

T dropped the Porsche key in Pixie's hand and walked away from her and out of the parking garage. He half expected to hear her voice screaming after him. But he heard nothing. He half expected to find her waiting for her when he got home. But she wasn't there.

I definitely won't be telling Alison anything about this, he vowed.

The next morning, T woke up to find the Porsche keys sitting on top of his Bose clock radio. It was six A.M., so it took him a second to fully register these were the keys he gave back to Pixie. But if he returned them to Pixie, how could the car keys have made it into his room? T felt a sudden chill of apprehension. He looked around his room. He stared at his bedroom windows. There was no sign any of his belongings had been disturbed. Everything looked the same this morning as it had the previous night. But now it was starting to seem to T that he had a stalker who was capable of disarming his home's security system.

I should probably tell Alison about this, he decided.

Alison remained silent for a moment after T haltingly recited the full horror of his Pixie trauma. The Chevy Impala drove for a block before she finally spoke.

"Take out that piece of paper," she said. T looked confused. "The piece of paper I gave you after your surprise visit to *Jen?*"

T dug around in his jacket pocket, produced the scrap of paper, unfolded it, and read, "I told you so."

Gazing out the window, Alison said, "I knew she had a thing for you. Right away, I could see it. But if I'd said anything, if I'd told you how crazy and obsessive she gets, you'd have called me jealous and immature, and we'd have ended up fighting. And I *really* wanted to be wrong."

T picked up speed. "She came to my *house*, Alison. You should have tried harder to tell me."

Alison's eyes flared. "You should have tried harder not to lead her on."

"I didn't do anything wrong," he protested.

"In what parallel universe?" she gasped. "You took a car from her. You were okay about accepting Lakers tickets from her. You spent a fun day with her."

"I thought we were working on the column."

Alison glared at T with derision.

He winced, suddenly aware how lame that must have sounded. Suddenly aware how lame he must have been to believe that Pixie was actually interested in having him write for her magazine.

"You did all this stuff with her. And you told me *nothing*!"

The Chevy Impala ran a red light. T swerved up a side street and attempted to catch his breath. "I screwed up," he admitted.

"Me too," said Alison. "Although, really, I didn't. I'm just saying that to make you feel better."

T brandished the "I told you so" note. "This isn't a screwup in your eyes?"

Alison glared at T. "I shouldn't *have* to tell my boyfriend not to go sneaking off to bowl with strange, needy, obsessive girls." They sat in angry silence for a moment. Then Alison said, "It's my mess. I'll fix it."

TWENTY-EIGHT

Irreconcilable Differences

$\mathcal{A}$*lison heard the* giggling from inside Pixie's Palace. The office door opened. Avril Lavigne's publicist backed out with the usual pained look on his face. Alison couldn't stop herself from peeking inside. New managing editor Cutesy Woo was luxuriating inside Pixie's inner sanctum, the besotted look of the suddenly included plastered all over her face. Pixie saw Alison lurking outside.

"Yes," she said like an aged countess addressing a lowly house-maid. "Was there something?"

Alison wanted to shout, "Leave my boyfriend alone!" but chose to wait for a more appropriate time. She shook her head and started to walk away.

"Then close my door," ordered Pixie. "And go back to . . .

whatever it is you do around here. Intern." Not so much as a suggestion that they'd ever been friends.

Alison shut the office door. The giggling continued.

Alison decided to take refuge in the interns' room while she waited for a private moment to confront Pixie. Amandine was sitting cross-legged in the middle of the room, patiently folding a towering pile of clothes that were to be boxed up and returned to the designers who loaned them out for shoots.

"You are an awesome beauty editor," Alison told Amandine. "You shouldn't be doing this."

The ex-editor didn't even look up from her task. She looked defeated. Nothing Alison could say would make the situation at *Jen* any less unhappy. Alison pulled an armful of clothes from the pile, sat down next to Amandine, and began folding.

By seven thirty that night, Alison was the sole folder in the intern room. She had become so caught up in the rhythm of the job that she failed to notice Pixie watching her from the doorway.

"Good little worker," she smirked, and then began to walk away.

Alison jumped up and began to go after her. "Hey, Pixie. Do you have a minute?" Pixie kept walking. Alison headed down the corridor after her. "Can I talk to you?" she repeated.

"I know you *can* because of the volume of your screechy voice," said Pixie without looking back. "The question is *may* you talk to me, and my answer is no."

Pixie's tone infuriated Alison. "Fine. *May* you leave my boyfriend alone?"

"I thought you didn't have a boyfriend," retorted Pixie, still not looking back.

"I said it was complicated. I thought you might be smart enough to understand that I meant it had nothing to do with you."

Pixie stopped by the reception desk and whirled around.

Wanting to both wound and console Pixie, Alison said, "I know you're lonely, and I know you're desperate to connect with people, but I can only sympathize up to a point. And that point is when you try to steal my boyfriend."

Pixie's eyes shrank down to black dots of loathing. Her fists balled. Color spread across her face. "He told me how much he hates you," she spat. "He feels sorry for you, that's the only reason he still goes out with you."

Alison stared at Pixie. *This just gets sadder and sadder*, she thought.

The pity in Alison's eyes pushed Pixie further over the edge. "He's coming to my sweet sixteen, you know that, right? *As my date*. He's dumping you *finally*. Like he's always wanted to. And he's going to be with me."

Alison thought back to the calm, measured tones of her former therapist, Dr. Mee. *Carmen may have mind controlled her into trying to kill me, but she was pretty good at her job.* "You know that's not true, Pixie. It's just something you wish would happen. But you have to accept that you can't get everything you want." Alison could see from the conflicting emotions flying across Pixie's face that the tiny girl was painfully aware how ridiculous she was sounding. *She's going to cry. And I'm going to have to hug her and tell her everything's okay*, predicted Alison gloomily.

But Pixie didn't cry. She broke into a harsh laugh. "God, you're *so* stupid, Alison. I could see that the day you showed up here in your stewardess outfit. But I thought there might be some hope for you. I thought I could help you. But you're beyond help. You're *so* dumb. Don't you understand that I *always get everything I want? Always!*"

Alison continued to channel Dr. Mee. "That's right, let it all out. Purge it from your system."

"You're so pathetic," snarled Pixie. "I don't even know what he sees in you."

Suddenly feeling a whole lot less empathetic, Alison shot back, "I don't know, either. Oh, wait, maybe I do." She began counting on the fingers of her left hand. "Let's see: One, I'm not a spoiled brat. Two, I don't have a million different personalities, each one more horrific than the last. And Three, I didn't turn my back on a bunch of girls who did nothing but love and support me."

A smile of pure evil split Pixie's face. "I haven't turned my back on them. As it happens, I've got big plans for those losers. I'm gonna put them in a cage, make them slug it out till there's only one intern left standing. Winner gets to keep her job. My money's on the Somali chick. She looks like she can take a lot of punishment."

Alison gaped at Pixie. "You're a monster," she said.

"You didn't think I was so bad when you begged me to take care of Treasure Spinney for you," retorted an unconcerned Pixie.

Alison reached out a hand and gripped onto the reception desk. She had a sudden premonition she was going to need to steady herself. "What do you mean?" Alison asked in a small, fearful voice.

Pixie pulled out her phone and pressed a key. A 3-D

holographic image of Ludovic Furmanovsky hung in the air. "Daddy," Pixie cooed to the image, "My friend Allywally hates Treasure Spinney. Kill her career, would you?" Pixie touched another key. The image disappeared. "He did it for me. And I asked him to do it for you. So, technically, you did it. You got her show canceled. You buried her CD. You made cats sick."

Alison felt her heart start pounding. "I don't believe you."

"Oh, it's true, baby," Pixie gloated. "And you know what? It was so much fun wrecking her career and ruining her life that from now on, I'm going to do it to *everyone* on the What's Not List. Anyone who incurs my royal displeasure is going to wind up clutching a tin cup and begging for spare change outside Starbucks. Thanks for the idea, Allywally." And then Pixie broke into a wide happy smile. She wasn't gloating now. She wasn't reveling in the despair of her victims. She was exhilarated.

"We really make a great team," gushed Pixie. "Oh, Alison, I hate all the fighting. Why don't we run this magazine together? You and me? Wouldn't it be cool? My daddy would totally approve!" Pixie trotted up to Alison and grabbed both her hands. The expression on her face was so open and warm that Alison was almost tempted. *My own magazine*, she couldn't help thinking. *Me, running* Jen. *I could get the old editors their jobs back. I could get rid of the blondes and Brazilians. I could stop Pixie from using the What's Not List for her personal vendettas. I could help her be normal. I could . . .*

"And I promise it wouldn't be weird for you seeing me and T together."

Alison stopped dreaming about running *Jen*. Her hands heated up.

Pixie screamed in pain. "You *burned* me!" she yelled, shoving her fingers in her mouth. The reception area was suddenly filled with onlookers. The security guards. The blondes and Brazilians. The ex-editors. Cutesy Woo holding up gummy shoes. "I hate you!" shrieked Pixie.

And then Alison had a moment of clarity. She looked at Pixie's scarlet, rage-spattered face. She looked at the blondes and Brazilians and the ex-editors and Cutesy Woo, and she suddenly realized, *None of this has anything to do with me. I can just walk away.* Once she realized that, Alison headed toward the elevators.

"I had fun working here," she said as she left the group of girls behind her. "But this isn't my favorite magazine anymore. So I quit."

As she stepped into the elevator, she heard Pixie roar, "You can't quit. You're *fired!*" The elevator began its descent from the twenty-third floor, but Alison could still hear Pixie's screams of rage echoing above her.

TWENTY-NINE
Reunited

Alison basked in the glow of her triumphant exit from *Jen* for approximately two hours. She was back in her bedroom, gleefully posting anti-*Jen* sentiments on the *Pink Sugar* message boards when she got the first of what would turn out to be many messages from her former employer.

"So sad you're not part of the fam anymore," said Pixie on Alison's iPhone. Even though Pixie pulled down her lower lip to emphasize how broken up she was over the unexpected exit of America's No. 1 *Jen* Girl, Alison didn't think she seemed all that unhappy. "But even though your sunny smile won't be brightening up the office any longer, I don't want to lose you as a reader. So stand by your phone, Allywally, 'cuz I'm going to be sending you exclusive sneak previews of all the awesome content coming up in the next issue."

Alison rolled her eyes at the image of Pixie on her phone.

"And *especially* our coverage of the tragic downfall of poor little Treasure Spinney. The stuff that happened to her before is *nothing* compared to what's coming next . . ."

The message ended with Pixie giving Alison a cute little wink. Alison had been winked at by Pixie before. It was not a pleasant experience. And then the follow-up messages began to trickle in. All of them hinting at new calamities about to befall Treasure Spinney. All of them hinting that Alison was complicit. As much as she wanted to dismiss the threats as the petulance of a spurned ex-friend turned borderline stalker, Alison started to suspect the worst. Which motivated her to start sending some messages of her own.

"*Jen's* run by a fifteen-year-old psycho who ruined Treasure Spinney's career 'cuz I asked her to!" Alison's blunt opening sentence made certain that the emergency Department of Hotness meeting she'd called was not marred by awkwardness or embarrassment. She looked around the empty cookery classroom that was acting as the location for their reunion gathering. Satisfied that Kellyn, David, Dorinda, and T were more interested in what she had to say than dwelling on the petty squabbles that had separated them, she held up her iPhone and told the assembled group about the first message Pixie had sent her. Then she passed the phone down the table so they could see the rest of her emails.

Alison looked at her estranged friends. "She's taunting me.

She's letting me know she's going to destroy Treasure Spinney. And she's trying to make me feel guilty for it."

"Celebrities melt down all the time," said Kellyn. "Actresses go haywire every second. It's the American way. Are you really gonna blame every bad thing that happens to Treasure Spinney on this Pixie chick? You might not like her, but do you really think she's capable of playing with people's lives to this extent?"

"Oh, *hell, yes!*" responded T with uncharacteristic passion.

Alison gave T a suspicious look. They hadn't discussed it since the heated drive to school a few days earlier, but they were both aware Alison still blamed T for not being fast enough in discouraging Pixie's advances.

Turning back to the others, Alison declared, "I am not a paranoid person. I trust people until they give me reason not to. She's given me reason not to."

Dorinda looked up from her BlackBerry. "She's got everything. Why would she want to hurt so many people?"

Alison leaned forward. "Because she doesn't have *anything*. Her daddy gives her whatever she asks for except his time and his attention. The less love he shows her, the more out of control she gets."

Kellyn shook her head in disgust. "Oh, *boo hoo*," she taunted. "No one loves me, so I'm going on a rampage. I can't get what I want, so everyone has to suf—" Kellyn stopped abruptly. She had become aware that what she was saying was too close to home. She darted the tiniest glance at Dorinda, who was staring at her BlackBerry, her lips pursed so tightly they were white.

David jumped in to fill the awkward silence. "So you're going to become Treasure Spinney's personal bodyguard?"

Alison shook her head. "Nope, I'm not. *We* are. The Department of Hotness. I did extensive research on T-Spin for what would have been my brilliant Oscar-winning cover story if she hadn't ruined it by being so completely vile and horrible. I know where she hangs out. I know where she hides away. I know her managers and her publicists and her numerologists and her psychologists and her vocal coach and her reflexologist. I reached out to my friend Amandine at *Jen*, and she got me Treasure's schedule. I know where she's going to be and who she's going to be with. I know her every stupid move. We're going to be her shadows. If anyone wants to put their hands on Treasure Spinney, they're gonna have to get through us. Which is not gonna happen! Because we're un-get-through-able!" Alison raised a suddenly burning hand in the air. "Let me hear you say, 'We're un-get-through-able!'"

T, Dorinda, and Kellyn looked at each other, each silently wondering if their friend had misplaced her marbles. But there was a big wide grin on David's face. He understood that Alison's superhero side had reasserted itself. His voice rang out loudest and most enthusiastic when the rest of the group dutifully chorused, "We're un-get-through-able!"

"That's right!" Alison was ablaze with righteousness and excitement. She was back with her old friends, she was going to ruin Pixie's evil plans, and she was about to set out on a brand-new *mish*!

THIRTY
The Mish

The following afternoon, the reunited Department of Hotness embarked on their mish to stop Pixie from wreaking further havoc on Treasure Spinney. In the case of Alison and Kellyn, they embarked on the mish by spending two and a half hours running in and out of the changing rooms of Miss Spinney's favorite vintage clothes emporium, Polkadots and Moonbeams on Third Street. Anyone watching the two girls emerging from the rooms clad in taffeta and leopard-print evening dresses and then dissolving into helpless laughter could have been forgiven for thinking—as the sales staff certainly did—that they were just a pair of giggling schoolgirls whiling away an afternoon. The sales staff were not entirely wrong. Alison and Kellyn had *completely* forgotten that they were on a mish.

"Oh My God," gasped Alison. "How dearly do I wish I had come here before my first day at *Jen?*"

"You really went to that office dressed as a stewardess?" Kellyn cackled. "That's, like, a step away from showing up in a chicken outfit. It makes my day when things go bad for you. I know it's wrong to say that, but I can't help it."

Alison was taken aback by how happy Kellyn had been all afternoon. Sure, they were having fun dressing up. Sure, she really did thrive anytime Alison was in distress. But there was something else. This was a brand of happiness Alison recognized. "You really like David, don't you? I mean *really* like him?"

Kellyn admired her leopard-skin dress in the mirror. Betraying no obvious emotion, she shrugged. "He's okay. He's funny, you know . . ." And then she couldn't stop herself. Reaching out an arm, she yanked the surprised Alison back into the changing room, pulled her close, and whispered into her ear, "I'm kind of crazy about him." Kellyn clamped a hand over her mouth as if she was trying to stop any more revelations from flying out.

Alison was amused by Kellyn's flustered state and happy for her happiness. But deep inside she couldn't help thinking, *That's what you look like when you're in love. I don't look like that anymore . . .*

According to Alison's schedule, Treasure Spinney generally left her favorite vintage clothes shop and made her way to Tiny Steps, a dance studio in Burbank. David had positioned himself outside the studio, pretending to be immersed in a comic book but making careful note of every figure who entered and left the building.

I'm an awesome undercover man, David found himself thinking. *I blend into the background. No one notices me, but I see everything. Maybe this is my calling. I might not have actual superpowers, but I've got my own particular skill set. I'm like the invisible man.*

"Excuse me," said a voice, jolting David back to reality. He found himself looking into the suspicious eyes of a tall thin woman wearing a leotard and ballet shoes. "You've been lurking out here for twenty minutes now. Can I ask what you're doing?"

Awesome undercover man David Eels found himself momentarily lost for words. His hesitancy brought a warmth to the woman's initially unfriendly demeanor.

"You don't have to say anything." She smiled. "It's written all over your face. You want to move. To fly free. To let the dancer inside you soar."

David opened his mouth to disagree with her assessment. The dance teacher suddenly had her hand under his elbow. She propelled him toward the studio. "I don't have a dancer inside me!" he tried to tell her. But she didn't seem to believe him.

Straight after her dance lesson, Treasure was scheduled to return to her bungalow at the Chateau Marmont for an hour of Me Time. T and Dorinda had been sitting across the pool from Treasure's rented home for almost an hour. They'd seen no sign of anything suspicious.

"She might be in disguise," suggested Dorinda. "You know what a brilliant actress she is. She could totally have slipped past us, and we wouldn't even notice."

Sipping at an ice coffee, T sighed. "Which would be yet another reason for Alison to be mad at me."

Dorinda looked up from her white-chocolate mocha. "*Excuse-*

moi? Brangelina Googles you guys for cuteness tips. What's she got to be mad at you for? Not being perfect enough?"

T said, "I guess you haven't been paying attention?"

Dorinda replied, "I guess you haven't been paying attention to what I'm paying attention to."

T gave her a sympathetic look. "We're all wrapped up in our little worlds. We don't notice what other people are going through. Are you okay?"

Dorinda looked surprised at T's unexpected compassion. She smiled at him. "Nope."

Neither of them spoke for a moment. Dorinda pulled out her deck of cards and began idly shuffling them.

"Wow," remarked T, taken aback by her dexterity. "You cut that deck with one hand."

"Did I?" mumbled Dorinda, who was barely paying attention.

"I didn't know you did card tricks," he said.

Dorinda looked pained. "That's funny. Because everyone usually pays *such close attention* to every little thing I say and do."

"I'm paying attention now," said T. "Show me what else you got."

So Dorinda showed him the Overhand Shuffle, the Hindu, and the Corgi. T was impressed by her sleight of hand. Dorinda was pleased to be performing in front of an appreciative audience. Neither one felt as miserable as they had when they first sat down. Then they took sips from their drinks, and Dorinda found herself thinking that this was the first time she had ever spent any time alone with T. And that he was *such* a sweet guy.

★ ★ ★

T was in a good mood. The mission had been a bust. Relations with Alison were frosty. But Dorinda had been fun to hang out with. Plus, he'd heard that an aggressive nine-year-old tap dancer had kicked David in the ear. So the smart and resourceful David Eels was screwing up his part of the mish? That, he couldn't deny, made him feel good. And that made the endorphins kick in. Which made his nightly run around Griffith Park that much more exhilarating.

His arms and legs were pumping in rhythm to the vintage Motörhead banging in his headphones (Alison's conversion to AC/DC had inspired T to reacquaint himself with *Ace of Spades*). His breathing was even. He felt the night wind fly past his face.

Further up the running path, someone stood motionless. T couldn't see whether the figure was a lost child or an exhausted runner fighting for breath. As he drew closer, the figure became clearer. He couldn't see a face or a body, but there was a person wearing what looked like a monk's cowl. T ran a few more yards. It was definitely *like* a cowl, but it was made from a sort of gold silk that seemed to shimmer in the night as if made from millions of tiny lights. T ran a few more steps The figure tossed its head and the hood fell back. It was Pixie.

T stopped running. He glanced around him. The running track was empty. There was no one else around. His heart was thumping. He tried not to let her see how freaked out he was. Pixie said nothing. Her arms were crossed over her chest. Her fingertips touched her shoulders. She looked up at him from beneath lowered eyes. T considered just running straight past her. Maybe if he showed Pixie he wasn't scared, she'd back off.

"Do you like my dress?' Pixie said.

T knew that this was a question that didn't have a reply that worked out well for him. If he said Yes, she'd take it as a sign that he liked her. If he said No, she'd go nuts. So he said nothing.

"I wore it for you," she said.

Oh, no, T thought.

Pixie let her arms drop. As she did, she opened them wide, and the gold silk fell like bat wings. T felt his mouth go dry. Pixie didn't take her eyes from his face. She stood with her arms extended *and then she began to slowly rise into the air.* T knew that this was the moment to run. This was the moment to yell for help. This was the moment to get as far away from her as he could. But he did nothing. He wasn't capable of speaking or moving. He just stared uncomprehendingly as Pixie continued to rise up into the air, until she floated four feet above his head.

"It's so nice to see you again," she murmured dreamily. "I always thought there was this electricity between us. I know you feel it, too." Then Pixie pointed a finger in the direction of T's chest. A bolt of electricity flew from the gold tendrils coiled around her fingers, slammed straight into T's chest, and knocked him unconscious.

THIRTY-ONE

T-Pain

God, I feel great, thought T drowsily. *There's nothing like waking up from a long, deep sleep. And this mattress feels fantastic. I never noticed the way it molds itself around me. And these sheets are so soft. I should say something to Birgit. I know she knows how much we appreciate everything she does for us, but it wouldn't hurt to actually come out and say the words.*

T blinked a few times and opened his eyes. He was not at home. This was not his room. This was twice the size of his room. And it was sleek and all white. It looked brand new and expensive and completely unlived in.

"I'm dreaming," T croaked to himself. "It happens most mornings. You think you're awake, but you're still dreaming." T dragged the sheets aside and sat up in bed, waiting to wake up.

"Good morning, sleepyhead," said a familiar voice.

T let a brief cry of fear escape. Then his eyes turned cold. Jumping from the bed, he ran to the white door and pulled hard. Nothing happened. He pulled harder. It wouldn't budge. Terror and adrenaline mixed inside T. He went from pulling at the door to aiming kicks at it. After a few useless attempts, he gave up and slumped down on the white floor, red-faced and gasping.

Pixie's giggles echoed around the room. "Someone's awful grouchy in the morning." She laughed.

Shaking with fear and fury, T looked up at the corners of the ceiling.

Sitting in the hidden surveillance room inside the library, Pixie watched multiple images of T fill the monitors. She pushed a button, and they all went into extreme close-up. She leaned her elbows on the control panel and put her hands on her cheeks like she was fondly gazing at the movie star of her dreams.

"Why are you doing this?" said T, trying hard to sound reasonable.

Pixie reached out a finger and touched the image of T's face on the nearest monitor. "Because I only got to have one day with you. And I want more."

T stared at the spot on the ceiling where, he imagined, cameras were concealed. "There's no way you can get away with this. I'll be missed."

"Of course you will." Pixie smiled. "*I* missed you. That's why I brought you here. So I wouldn't have to miss you anymore."

Panic spread across T's face. "What do you think my family is going to do?"

Pixie bounced up and down in her chair. "Ooh, I can totally

answer that. I can even tell you what they're doing right this min-ute. They're boarding a Cathay Pacific flight to Tokyo. It's so awesome that I get to be the one to tell you. Last night, your dad got an amazing offer. The Sony corporation wants to buy his speaker company. So amazing that he and the Swedish step-mommy are flying first class to meet the bigwigs. That's a funny word, isn't it? *Bigwigs*."

"You're lying," said T. "My dad's company is worth millions."

Pixie wrinkled her nose. "What, two, *three* million? That's so cute. But they're offering him *miiiiillions*. So he's got other things on his mind than who's taking care of his little boy. Which, by the way, I am . . ."

T stared wildly around the room. The endless unbroken whiteness was eating at him even more than Pixie's voice. There had to be a way out of here. "Alison's going to find out," he said.

Pixie shook her head. "I don't think she will," she said. "Right now, she's too busy running around trying to save Treasure Spinney. She hasn't worked out that I had a fake schedule sent to her so she'd be out of my way when I came for you. She'll put two and two together in the end. She's just about smart enough to accomplish that. But not before you and I have had so much fun that I bet you won't even want to go back to her."

Pixie's laugh echoed around the room. T put his hands over his ears, but even then he could still hear it.

I'm so completely over T, scowled Alison as she looked around the cafeteria for signs of her elusive boyfriend. She'd called him the previous night. No reply. She'd emailed and texted before she went to sleep. Not a word. And then this morning before school, more calls and texts. More nothing in return. *Is he just avoiding me?* she wondered. *Is this the non-confrontational dump? He can't do that to me. I deserve to be confrontationally dumped.* Alison's annoyance leapt up a few notches when she saw Lark Rise sit down at a table with her band of earnest juniors. *Don't go up to Lark Rise and ask her if she's seen T,* a voice inside Alison implored her. *It'll only make you mad if she's talked to him and you haven't. So don't do it.*

Alison agreed with the voice but still found herself unable to stop herself from walking toward the junior table. "Hi, Lark," she mumbled.

Lark replied by rattling a tin can with an "SOS" label under her nose. "Save Our Sea lions. Stop the trawling," said Lark.

Alison stared uncomprehendingly for a moment. Lark rattled the can again. Alison heard the jangle of coins inside. She nodded and felt inside her bag for change. As she groped inside her purse, she said, as casually as she could manage, "You haven't seen T in your travels, have you?" Alison dropped a few dimes and Tic Tacs inside Lark's sea lion can and gave the girl what she hoped wasn't a look of pathetic hopelessness.

"That *boy!*" Lark exclaimed. "I was just saying to Birgit last night, he's never there when you need him. It's almost like he enjoys making you wonder where he is and what he's doing. Let *me* know if you find him. We've got lots to talk about." And with that, Lark went back to her group of juniors.

Didn't I say you'd be mad? said the voice inside Alison as she stomped out of the cafeteria and walked straight into Dorinda.

"What's wrong with?—" Dorinda almost got a chance to ask before Alison interrupted her.

"Lark Rise should *not* have a special relationship with T's stepmom," complained Alison. "If anyone should have a special relationship with her, it's me. T should just *know*. He just should just know what's okay and what's not okay."

"What's going on with you two?" asked Dorinda.

"Nothing." Alison sighed. "That's the problem. I think we're over."

T didn't know how long he'd been sitting on the floor, his arms around his knees. He was trying to let the fear subside and think rationally. Despite what Pixie said, his family would miss him, his friends would miss him, and the school would miss him. The police would get involved. Pixie's father, wealthy and powerful as he was, would not want his name touched by scandal. Pixie might be crazy, but from what Alison had said, she would not want to risk incurring his displeasure. When it came down to it, Pixie was a spoiled little girl who was entirely committed to having everything she wanted. And the thing with spoiled little girls who get everything they want is that as soon as they get it, they always want something else. T started to feel a little hopeful.

And, at that moment, the door slid slowly open. T sat and watched it for a moment. It had only opened a few inches. But it wasn't locked anymore. T thought, *This is her way of telling me she wants me to leave without making a fuss. Just disappear and act like nothing ever happened.*

"I've already forgotten," he said, jumping to his feet. T walked across the white floor and grabbed the door handle. The electricity that suddenly ran up his arms and through his body made his limbs flail wildly for a second before he was hurled backward onto the floor.

Pixie walked into the room. She looked at T, shivering on the ground. She wasn't wearing her dress, but the gold tendrils were still around her fingers. Electricity crackled around the coils. Pixie stretched a languid hand out toward the shaking T. "Tell me I'm pretty," she said.

THIRTY-TWO
Shocked

$\mathcal{A}lison's\ four\text{-}bell$ ringtone tolled ominously.

"*Finally,*" she said.

"Mr. T?" asked Kellyn. She was sprawled across the floor of Alison's bedroom as they studied Treasure Spinney's schedule in preparation for their next few days of shadowing.

"Only a whole entire day after I called him," she muttered, staring at his face on the iPhone.

"He left you dangling. Do the same to him. Be the dangler."

Alison clicked the phone off. "I will be the dangler," she vowed.

The white room smelled of burning. T was quivering and sweating. His eyes were wild and his limbs twitched independently of him.

"One last thing, sweetie, then we're done, then we can relax and have fun," said Pixie. "Tell her you never want to see her again." She held up her *pixie*Phone. T hesitated for a split second. Pixie pointed her finger. Electricity crackled around the gold tendrils.

"I never want to see you again," he gasped.

Pixie pressed "Send." Then she clicked her phone off. "And we're done." She smiled at T and waggled her fingers. He cowered in fear. "If only I'd had these when I was trying to train my Little Pixie. He'd have been so obedient. Alison would never have been able to steal him away from me. Still, I guess things worked out for both of us. But better for me, of course. Always better for me."

Ten minutes later, Alison was in the bathroom when the first bell of her ringtone boomed out. T calling again.

"Be the dangler!" yelled Kellyn.

But Alison's dangling powers quickly deserted her. She went to check the message. She saw T's face. It was drenched in sweat. He was twitching. He looked like he'd seen a ghost. His lips started to move.

Alison wasn't affected by what he was saying. She could hear the words "I never want to see you again." But it was the way he was saying them. Like he was a hostage. Like he was being forced to say them. Like he'd been hurt. "Oh God," gasped Alison. And then her hands started shaking as she went to replay the other messages she'd ignored:

"I never liked you. I only felt sorry for you."

"I never thought you were pretty."

"I hate everything about you."

Alison's legs gave out. She slumped down onto the floor of the bathroom.

"You okay in there? You're dangling, right?" Kellyn laughed from inside the bedroom.

"Kel," whispered Alison. She couldn't speak. She couldn't get the words out.

Once more, the phone rang. Pixie's face appeared. It took Alison two hands to hold the phone.

She read the text: "We're having the funnest day ever. I want 2 tell u all about it. B at Jen 2night. 8. Tell no 1. ☺ xxx P"

Alison stared at the text. Tears poured down her face. *I let this happen. I was mad at him. And she took him. And she hurt him.*

THIRTY-THREE

I Killed a Girl and I Liked It

The elevator doors opened. Alison stepped out on the twenty-third floor clad in full Hottie regalia. *I need to feel strong. I need her to know who I really am and what I can do.* She checked her watch. It was eight exactly. Most nights at this time, *Jen* was still buzzing. But not tonight. No blondes or Brazilians. No sobbing interns. Nothing. *Jen* was deserted and dark. The bedazzled desk glinted and sparkled in the gloom. Alison waited in the reception area for a second. Her every instinct warned her to exercise maximum caution. *This is obviously a trap.* But Alison was also painfully aware that Pixie had the upper hand. She had T. So Alison had no option but to proceed slowly through the *Jen* offices.

The teen idols captured in the plasma covers winked and

smiled at her, their airbrushed faces and shiny teeth gleaming like stars in the darkness. And then she reached Pixie's Palace.

Bowling Ball Face and Green Lightning Bolt Head stood guard on either side of the white door. They displayed no emotion at the sight of Alison. They had no reaction to her attire.

"I've got an appointment," she said.

"We need to frisk you," replied Bowling Ball Face.

"Frisk me?" repeated Alison.

"Pat you down," explained Green Lightning Bolt Head. "Check you for concealed weapons."

"Boss's orders," pointed out Bowling Ball Face.

"I bet," said Alison.

"Make it easy on yourself," said Green Lightning Bolt Head, drawing himself up to his full six foot plus.

"Face the wall and spread your arms. We won't be too rough." Bowling Ball Face let the hint of a grin break up the monotony of his features.

Alison stood her ground. Both men started to move away from the white door. As they got closer, Alison looked at Bowling Ball Face and asked, "You still got that eyebrow pencil?"

Before the word *why* escaped his open mouth, Alison aimed both middle fingers at him. A second later, he was standing in stunned silence, his hands feeling around the tender patches above his eyes where hair once grew. She turned her attention to Green Lightning Bolt Head.

"I know it probably doesn't seem like it, but I'm about to do you the favor of your life." She aimed her fingers.

Green Lightning Bolt Head was about to throw his hands up to protect his fancy emerald Mohawk. He was too late. By the time his hands touched his scalp, all he could feel was a strip of hot green stubble.

"That's *so much better!*" exclaimed Alison as she perused her handiwork. "Now, why don't you face the wall and *I'll* frisk you?"

The two guards stared at the flames that were now engulfing Alison's open hands. Then they pushed and shoved each other as they scrambled to be the one that got furthest away from the door. Alison watched them run. Once they'd vanished from view, she turned back to the white door of Pixie's Palace.

"Come," said the voice from inside.

The lights were off in Pixie's office, but the glow from her gold dress filled the room. Alison struggled to see a face inside the shimmering shape. She could make out the tiny flashing lights and sensors threaded through the gold silk, but there was just blackness beneath the hood.

"Allywally," said Pixie from her throne.

"Pixie Stix," hissed Alison.

Pixie shook her head with amusement as she gazed at Alison's Hottie costume. "Another winner from that closet of yours." Then her smile grew more genuine. "I was right about you, wasn't I? You're this pretty, perfect LA blonde, but you're *so* not. There's so much more going on with you. But I guess I never knew *how much more*. Friends shouldn't keep secrets from each other, Alison. Especially when they're this hot . . ."

"*What did you do to him?*" Alison interrupted, her voice cracking. Not being able to see Pixie's face was unnerving her. She felt her fingers heating up.

"I made him pay attention," said Pixie. "I made him see that I was the only girl in the world."

Alison felt herself go weak. She attempted to reason with Pixie. "You can't do this. T's a popular guy . . ."

"He's popular with me." Pixie laughed.

"Everyone's going to notice he's gone," said Alison. "His family, his friends, the school . . ."

Pixie yawned in the darkness. "I've been through all this stuff with T. *He* seemed to grasp it easily enough. His family's out of the picture. And as far as his friends and the school go . . ."

The chandelier in the office ceiling suddenly blazed to life. Alison had to shield her eyes. She heard a familiar voice say, "I've taken care of that." When her eyes swam back into focus, Alison saw Lark Rise reclining on a huge cushion, an open magazine in her lap. "It worked out really well, Alison," said Lark brightly. "I've got *so* many projects, as you know, and T was great about getting involved. So whenever anyone asks if I've seen him, I just tell them he's helping me with one of my *things*, and they totally buy it."

Alison felt like she was going to faint. "But . . . but you *like* him."

Lark nodded enthusiastically. "Love him. Such an awesome guy. *Way* too good for you."

Alison gestured to Pixie, whose face she could now see. "But . . . but . . . you want to save sea lions, and *she* . . ." Alison searched for an example of Pixie's heinousness. "Dogs fear her."

Lark shrugged, unfazed. "We've got different philosophies. But I practice tolerance. And, besides, she bought me my own magazine."

With a flourish, Lark brandished the magazine in her lap. The logo said, "*Lark*." The glamorously airbrushed shot on the front was of Lark. *T totally called it*, Alison thought, *like O, but L*.

"This is just a dummy," said Lark. "But the actual first edition is going to be incredible. We're going to explore issues in a way that's not just informative but fun—"

"No, *this* is just a dummy," interrupted Pixie, who pointed a tendril-coiled finger at Lark and shot a blast of electricity at her.

Lark opened her mouth one last time and then slumped unconscious into the open pages of her magazine.

"Can't stand her." Pixie sighed. She got up from her throne and walked out from behind her glittery desk to face a stunned Alison. "See, you're so much cooler than any of these other stupid girls I wasted my time trying to be friends with. That's why I keep breaking my own rules and giving you more chances. And now we get to be superheroes together! How fun is that?"

Alison stared at Pixie's fingers. Pixie made a V sign. The electricity crackled around the gold tendrils.

"How?" she said.

"Oh, Alison," smiled Pixie, as if talking to a child. "You've seen what my daddy's nerd factory can do."

Alison kept her eyes on the volts of electricity surging around Pixie's fingers.

"Did you do that to T? Did you use that on him?"

"You know what guys are like," Pixie laughed. "Sometimes they need to be trained like dogs. You give them a treat if they do what you want. And if they're naughty, you give them a . . ." Pixie wiggled her fingers and giggled as the electricity sparked and flashed.

Alison screamed in fury and blasted two jets of flame straight at Pixie. She didn't care if she hurt the girl. She didn't care what happened.

"First thing in the A.M., I'm calling my daddy and getting an upgrade," said Pixie. "'Cuz that? Was awesome."

Alison gaped at her. She was completely unhurt. Her beautiful gold silk dress was completely unmarked.

Pixie imitated the look of incomprehension on Alison's face. Then she started counting on her fingers. "One, I can fly. Two, I'm fireproof. Three, I'm way more powerful than you." She gave Alison her smuggest smile. "Scared yet?"

Alison balled her fists. They caught fire.

Pixie nodded. "So I guess we're fighting, huh? And over a guy! Hilarious! It's like something on TV." Amused, Pixie put a hand on her hip and wagged a warning finger in Alison's face. "No, you di-in't," she drawled. "Not with my man. Uh-uh."

Pixie's lightheartedness stabbed at Alison. She threw two fireballs straight at her giggling nemesis. The fireballs set Pixie's throne alight. They missed Pixie because she was suddenly floating in the air. Hanging a few feet below the chandelier, she smiled down at the shaken Alison.

"Four, faster than you. Five, smarter than you." And then electricity blasted from her fingers.

Alison ducked as the cushions on either side of her exploded. The thick, white shag carpet started giving off smoke and then caught fire. Alison thrust both hands into the air and shot flames at her enemy.

Pixie spread her arms and let the jets of fire hit her silken bat wings and then fall away into nothing. "They're flame retardant," explained Pixie of her wings. "Much like you, but with an extra *ant* at the end."

Alison whimpered with sudden fear. She'd expected a trap. But she hadn't expected Pixie to be more powerful than her. She hadn't expected her to be *invincible*.

Pixie sensed Alison's shock. "Aww," she pouted. "Is that *it*? Is that our fight? I expected more. Well, I don't know about you, but I feel better now we've both got that out of our systems. Now maybe we can talk like grown-ups." Pixie made a graceful descent from the ceiling. As she came halfway down to the ground, she whispered, "Allywally?"

Alison looked up. Pixie's black-leather Martin Margiela cut-out boots were level with her face. "You set my throne on fire!" she yelled. "You stole my dog! You think this fight is over?" Then she kicked out. *Hard*.

Alison reeled backward. She couldn't see straight. Her ears were ringing. Her mouth was *throbbing*.

Pixie landed directly in front of Alison. "That's gonna leave a scar. You might consider plastic surgery."

Alison gave Pixie the finger.

"Classy," mocked Pixie.

A blast of fire shot out of Alison's finger. A second later, the chandelier fell from the ceiling and knocked Pixie to the ground. "Lights-out," quipped Alison through a mouthful of blood.

A hand touched her shoulder. Alison screamed.

"It's me!" said Cutesy Woo. The new managing editor saw Pixie lying motionless under the chandelier She saw the bruises on Alison's face. "Oh My God," Cutesy whispered.

"She's crazy," gulped Alison, trying to get her breath back. "She tried to kill me. And she's got my boyfriend."

"Let's go to my office," said Cutesy.

As panicked as Alison was, Cutesy's sweet-scented serenity had a calming effect on her. She let herself be guided away from the smoking wreckage of Pixie's Palace.

Cutesy put her arm around Alison as they hurried down the dark corridor and through the reception area, finally pushing open her office door.

Like the rest of *Jen*, Cutesy's office was darkened. But her dazzling view of nighttime Los Angeles filled the room with light.

Alison slumped down behind Cutesy's desk. "I saw this coming," she found herself muttering. "But I was so wrapped up in being the one who got to say, 'I Told You So,' I did nothing. I let T get hurt."

"Don't dwell on what you can't change," counseled Cutesy Woo, who then began to whirl around her office, lighting candles.

The calming scents of bougainvillea, sea lily, and sandalwood filled the air. Cutesy touched a finger to her iPod dock. The sound of the ocean lapped gently around the office. Alison's jangled nerves began to calm.

"Relax," suggested Cutesy in a soothing whisper. "Let it all fade away."

Alison inhaled the mixed aromas of the candles that, she now noticed, took up every inch of floor and shelf space in Cutesy's office. The powerful scents and the insinuating sound of the ocean began to lull Alison toward sleep. Her head dropped down into her folded arms. She was seconds away from drifting away when she heard Cutesy Woo's voice.

"GET HER!!!"

Amandine charged into Cutesy's office holding a fire extinguisher. Alison fought her way back to full consciousness. She struggled to take in what she was seeing. Her friend. Running toward her. Carrying a fire extinguisher. Pointing it straight at her.

"DO IT!" Cutesy Woo was ordering Amandine. "FOAM HER AND THEN BLUDGEON HER UNCONSCIOUS!"

Alison whipped out a finger and shot a burst of flame at the fire extinguisher. The red canister immediately heated up. Amandine yelped in pain. She dropped the fire extinguisher, which fell on her foot. She yelped even louder. Then she caught sight of Alison's disappointed, disapproving face and immediately crumpled into a sobbing heap on the ground.

"I didn't want to do it, Alison," she wailed. "But Pixie promised me my job back if I gave you the fake Treasure Spinney schedule." Amandine started to swallow hard. Tears dribbled down her cheeks. "Then she said I needed to pass a loyalty test."

"By bludgeoning me?" asked Alison incredulously.

"I wasn't ever going to bludgeon you," Amandine sobbed. "I would have pummeled you, at best."

Alison shook her head at the wretched weeping heap who had once been her friend. But she wasn't so consumed with the declined-and-fallen Amandine that she didn't notice Cutesy Woo attempting to slink silently out of her office door. Alison shot a jet of fire at two clumps of Cutesy's exotic candles. They melted into a river of blazing wax that burned in a circle around Cutesy's ankles. She let out a squeal of fear.

"How are you doing that?" gasped Amandine.

"I'm America's No. 1 *Jen* Girl," muttered Alison. Then she picked up the remote control from Cutesy's desk. Alison aimed the remote. The far wall split into two. Cutesy's shoe racks appeared. They were illuminated at night. Even more impressive. "Where's my boyfriend?" asked Alison calmly.

"I don't know," peeped Cutesy defiantly.

Alison leaned back in Cutesy's Eames chair and pointed a finger at her shoe racks. The row of Marc Jacobs low-heel gauchos, Kate Spade ballet flats, and Juicy Couture Cameron T-strap flats went up in flames.

Cutesy's mouth dropped open. She gaped in shocked silence as her shoe collection was reduced to a burning mass.

"Where's my boyfriend?" asked Alison a second time.

"I told you, I don't know," said Cutesy, her voice shaking.

Alison pointed again. Cutesy's Manolo Blahnik alligator boots caught fire. She screamed.

"Stop!" she begged. "All I care about is my shoes!"

Alison immolated Cutesy's Louis Vuitton ostrich-leather boots. Cutesy let out a piteous "Waaaaaa!"

"*Where's my boyfriend?*" asked Alison. "Last chance for the Ferragamos."

"Tell her!" screamed Amandine.

Cutesy looked like she was fighting an internal battle. Finally, she nodded and hung her head.

Alison looked over at the shaking Amandine. "Foam her," she commanded.

Amandine gingerly picked up the still-hot fire extinguisher and blasted it at the burning mass of candle wax surrounding Cutesy.

Alison got up and sat on the edge of Cutesy's desk. "I'm waiting," she said.

The exquisite ex-receptionist stared down at the foam that had collected around her ankles. She looked up and, for the first time, made an attempt to speak in a clear, audible voice.

"Everyone got to go to the beach house," she managed to say. "Everyone got to go to Paris and Disneyland. Everyone except me. All I ever wanted was to be part of the family. But Pixie was so hung up on having her real girls around her. I was never included in anything. It was like I didn't exist. . . ."

Alison could see that Cutesy was letting out some long-pent-up emotions. But she really didn't care. "Right." She nodded. "So about my boyfriend . . ."

Tears that sparkled like diamonds spilled from Cutesy's turquoise eyes in perfect parallel lines. "When Pixie made me managing editor, I was so happy to finally be part of the group, I was willing to do anything she told me. . . ."

Amandine scrambled to her feet. She made her way over to Cutesy. "That's how it was for me when Pixie offered me a chance to get my old job back. It's like I didn't know the difference between right and wrong anymore. I would have done *anything.*"

Cutesy nodded gratefully at Amandine's display of empathy.

Alison coughed loudly to get the attention of the two emotional girls. They didn't seem to hear her. Amandine reached out and held Cutesy's hands. "I didn't know you felt like you were being left out. I'm so sorry. I wish you would have come with us to the beach house. We can totally hang out now if you'd like."

Cutesy smiled shyly. "I'd love that," she whispered. The two girls embraced.

"Where's my boyfriend!" shouted an infuriated Alison.

Cutesy gave Alison an apologetic smile. She opened her mouth to speak. A blast of electricity blew the office door off its hinges. The door smashed into Cutesy and Amandine, knocking them unconscious.

"Why do I hear talking?" screamed Pixie's voice from the hallway. "If I hear talking, that means Alison is still in one piece . . . AND THAT. IS NOT. WHAT I WANT!"

Alison looked frantically around the office for somewhere to hide. *In the shoe racks? Under the desk? Behind the candles?*

Pixie's taunting voice echoed from outside the office. "Do you want me to give you a minute to find somewhere safe to hide from me, Allywally? In this office I had built *from my own specifications*? But I'll play along if that's what you want. I'll count while you hide. Sixty . . . fifty-nine . . . fifty-eight . . . found somewhere yet? If you climb up on Cutesy Woo's desk, you can push open a ceiling panel and squeeze into the air vents. I'd never find you in there . . . fifty-seven . . ."

Alison couldn't think straight. Pixie's mocking voice drove her crazy. *I can't outthink her. I can't outpower her. I can't hurt her. She's got T. She's won. There's nothing I have that she doesn't.*

". . . fifty-three . . . fifty-two . . . fifty-one . . ."

Alison began to succumb to her fears. And then she realized she had one thing that Pixie didn't.

". . . forty-eight . . . forty-seven . . . forty-six . . ."

Alison sat back down at Cutesy's desk. She pulled out her phone and touched the screen.

"Hi, Dad," she said into the phone. She listened, smiled, and then pouted. "What, I can't just phone 'cuz I want to talk to my dad, see how he's doing, what sort of old-guy mischief he's getting up to?" Alison lay back in the chair and listened to her father's voice. "Nothing much," she said. "Just hanging out with friends. Hey, you know what you said about us having a *thing* that we do together? Yeah, like learning Italian or taking up sailing. Except not. None of those. How about Ally Picks The Movie Day? How about that?"

As Alison chatted to her father like she didn't have a care in the world, she saw Pixie walk slowly into the doorway of Cutesy's office. Her hands hung limply at her sides. She had a look of longing on her face. She didn't even acknowledge that Cutesy and Amandine were lying tangled in an unconscious heap on the ground.

Alison chuckled into the phone. "That's right! You have no say! *No say!* I pick the movies. We go to the movies. We come home. Activity!"

Pixie sat down on the ground and looked lost.

"Did I mention that I've come to really love those long, slow Eastern European movies, the ones in black and white with subtitles? Where a man walks down a street, looking for his lost donkey?" Alison giggled into the phone.

Pixie gazed at her. The yearning to belong was written all over her face.

"Okay, I gotta go. See you at breakfast." Alison clicked the phone off. Then she got up from Cutesy's desk and began to make her way out of the office.

"Are you really close with your dad?" Pixie's voice was a timid whisper.

Alison nodded. "He tries too hard to be funny. But otherwise I have no complaints."

"Maybe I could come to your house sometime? Maybe I could meet him?"

Keep walking, Ally, she told herself. *You've almost made it out of here in one piece.*

"That would be fun," said Alison, passing Pixie and putting a foot outside the doorway.

"Can you call him and ask him?" Pixie gazed up at Alison, a pleading look on her face. "Maybe we could all go see a movie? Or you could come to my house. Our screening room is awesome."

Oh God, thought Alison. "Sure," she agreed. "I'll ask him tomorrow morning. Over breakfast."

"Can I come home with you? We could have breakfast together? We could both ask him?"

OH GOD! thought Alison. "Well . . ." she began, "that would be fun, but I've got this test—"

"Or maybe . . ." interrupted Pixie, "maybe I'll just cause his old heart to explode in his chest." Pixie jumped to her feet. Her face was scarlet. Her eyes were shrinking. "HOW STUPID DO YOU THINK I AM? DO YOU THINK I WOULD WANT TO SET FOOT IN YOUR DIRTY SMELLY HOUSE? HOW DARE YOU THINK FOR A MINUTE THAT I'D WANT ANYTHING YOU'VE GOT. MY DADDY GIVES ME EVERYTHING!"

Well, that brilliant plan went south, thought Alison glumly. Lashing out, she burned a ring of fire around Pixie and ran from the office.

She almost made it to reception area when she felt the burst of electricity. Alison screamed in pain and fell to the ground.

Pixie strolled casually toward her. "No more last chances, Alison. I tried harder with you than with anyone. But I don't want to be friends with you anymore."

Alison was gripped by fear. Pixie was nuts. She was lethal and she was completely unpredictable. Summoning up all the courage she could muster, Alison pushed herself to her feet and rushed to the elevator door. She jammed a burning finger into the button. The door opened. Alison exhaled with relief. Electricity scraped at the air around her head as she fell inside. As the doors closed, she could hear Pixie's laughter. She saw her reflection in the elevator doors. Her hair was standing on end.

"That's a good look for you, Ally!" Pixie's voice called down from above.

Alison felt herself slump to the ground. Her tough exterior was gone. She closed her eyes for a second. The elevator juddered to a halt. Alison opened her eyes. She was stuck between the eighteenth and seventeenth floors. She got up to press the "Help" button.

Pixie's voice, faint but audible, echoed down the elevator shaft. "Hey, Ally, have you ever melted an elevator cable before? I'm just asking 'cuz you've had your powers longer than me. I'm blasting away and it doesn't seem to be moving . . ."

Alison felt her heart start beating. The elevator started to lurch.

"Okay, I think I got it. *Thanks! Bye!*"

The elevator began to plunge downward. Alison screamed in fear. The elevator fell faster.

16 . . . 15 . . . 14

Alison lost her balance. Her stomach was in her mouth. She felt herself being hurled around the elevator as if she were a pinball. Summoning up all the self-control she had left, Alison threw her arms in the air and burned a hole in the roof of the falling elevator. She dropped her arms by her sides, squeezed her fists together, shut her eyes, and screamed.

Two blasts of fire shot out from her fists, propelling her upward and through the hole in the elevator roof. Eyes still shut, she flew up the elevator shaft.

25 . . . 26 . . . 27

A loud crash from below opened her eyes. The elevator had smashed into the basement and exploded into debris.

Pixie's voice rang out, "Well, I hope America's *Next* No. 1 *Jen* Girl works out better."

Then her laughter faded away from the shaft.

Don't look down, Alison told herself. And immediately looked down. The wreckage of the elevator made her moan in terror. Then she looked back up and saw the roof of the shaft approaching. Praying that she had enough firepower in one arm, she kept her left arm pointing down, propelling her ever higher. She pushed her right hand into the air and shot out a burst of flame. Nothing. "COME ON!" she screamed. The blaze grew in power. The night sky appeared at the top of the elevator shaft. Alison squeezed her eyes shut, gritted her teeth, and flew through the hole in the roof of the big glass building in Century City.

THIRTY-FOUR

Survivor

"*Hiii, Mr. Cole,* it's Kellyn. Alison's friend? How are you? How's law? Sued anyone interesting? Listen, the reason I'm calling is your annoyingly perfect daughter's at my house, and we've been studying so hard the poor little thing's almost asleep. She's snoring and drooling—it's a delight. So I was thinking, it would be for the best if she stayed over at my place tonight? Is that cool? Thanks, Mr. Cole. She's really dead on her feet. Bye . . ."

Kellyn slipped her phone into her pocket. Some parts of what she'd told Roger Cole were true. Alison *was* almost asleep, and she *was* going to spend the night at Kellyn's house. Kellyn didn't think he needed to be bothered with the other stuff. The minor details about her calling him from the roof of the big glass building in Century City. Where Alison was bruised, banged up, and barely conscious. Where she had managed to crash-land on the surface of a huge satellite dish just before her powers began to taper off.

Kellyn didn't tell Alison's dad that David, Dorinda, and Designated Dean were carefully lifting his daughter's limp body down from the dish. She didn't think he needed to know that they were debating whether to take Alison straight to the emergency room but that her groaning protestations that she was okay convinced them she would be best looked after by her friends.

Two hours later, Alison was in the Hollywood Hills, tucked into Kellyn's mother's vast bed. She slowly, painfully dragged her eyes open. The first thing she saw was her reflection in the mirrored ceiling.

"How do you feel?" asked her assembled group of friends.

Alison considered the question. She'd had a bath. She'd swallowed a few painkillers. Dorinda had applied concealer to the bruises around her mouth. But she still felt ringing in her ears. Her scalp still tingled from the aftereffects of electric shock. She still ached in places she'd never ached before. And she had a strong urge to raise a finger and scorch her battle-scarred mirror image until it stopped staring down at her. *But . . .* for someone who started the evening facing certain death at the hands and feet of an all-powerful psychopath, she felt surprisingly chipper.

"Pixie didn't kill me," Alison finally replied. "She's stronger than me. She can fly. She's fireproof, and she's madder than a hundred Hatters. She beat me up. She scared me. She electric shocked me. She dropped me down an elevator shaft. But she couldn't kill me. She's not invincible. She's vincible. And I'm gonna vince her. And I'm gonna get T back."

"You're gonna get a tea bag?" asked Designated Dean, who had been going through Kellyn's mother's dresser drawers and was only half listening to the conversation.

David sat on the edge of the bed. "What if it was just a fluke she didn't kill you? What if you just got lucky and you used up your last allocation of luck?"

Alison gave him a surprised look. "Well, Little Mr. Sunshine, that's a chance I'm gonna have to take."

"You're not taking it alone," said Kellyn.

"I'm so mad at you for not calling us," shouted Dorinda. "You knew I always wanted to see the *Jen* offices. And you don't go on a mish without us. We're a team."

Alison rolled onto her side to face Dorinda. "Really? Is that what we are? Because it hasn't felt like that for a while."

"We've been a team of idiots," admitted Dorinda. "And we might still be a team of idiots." She shot a look at Kellyn. For once, it wasn't an antagonistic look. It was more of a I-know-I-went-too-far look. "But we're *your* idiots. And you're ours."

"Wow," said Alison, taken aback by her friend's passion.

"Doubly wow," echoed Kellyn.

"I'm out," said Designated Dean.

The others stopped talking and stared at him. He was overweight and unshaven. His upper right arm used to be tattooed with the word *Kaya*. But since the dancer who was once the object of his affections had neglected to let him know she had changed her number, he had Magic Markered an extra *k* to the end of the name. His sweatpants were worn at the knees and the crotch.

But on his face was something no one had ever seen before. An expression of deep concern.

The older boy suddenly felt self-conscious. Needing something to do with his hands, he pulled a black object from an open drawer and twisted it around his wrists as he talked. "I drive. I don't ask questions. But this is retarded. You're saying, 'She didn't kill me,' like it's a good reason to go back and give this wacko another chance."

"She's got T, Dean," said Alison.

"So call those guys . . ." He kept stretching the black object around his hands. "You know, the ones who drive the cars and wear the uniforms . . . They get to carry guns . . ."

"The cops?" suggested David.

"Them," nodded Double D. "This is too big for a bunch of kids. And that's all you are. And if something happens to you, I'm the one that's gonna have to . . ." He trailed off, embarrassed.

Alison bit her lip. She looked at the others and clutched her heart. "That's *so* sweet," she gushed. "Hugs for Double D!"

Immediately, Kellyn, Dorinda, and David leapt from the bed and embraced Designated Dean, who shoved them away. "All right, I'm not out," he muttered. "But I keep the car if something happens."

Dorinda and David went back to Alison.

Kellyn grinned ruefully at Double D. "Weird when that happens, huh? When you find yourself caring?" A nod of understanding passed between them. Kellyn returned to the huge bed. Without looking back at Designated Dean, she said, "Put my mom's bra back in the drawer when you're done with it, 'kay?"

★ ★ ★

T made it to the last of his one hundred push-ups and collapsed face-first on the all-white floor. He had determined he wasn't going to be a victim. He may have been trapped. He may have been tormented. But he wasn't going to roll into a ball and submit to Pixie. He was going to focus on getting stronger. So he stopped looking at the white room as a prison cell and started to see it as a gym. He devised a routine for himself. He started doing jumping jacks to warm himself up. Then he did a series of lunges. Then squat thrusts. Then sit-ups. He was going to be mentally and physically at his peak, and he was going to find a way out of here.

The door to the white room opened.

I'm bigger than she is. I'm stronger and I'm faster. If I have to hurt her, that's what I'm gonna do, he decided.

But it wasn't Pixie. Three men entered the room. Tall, well-built professional types just doing a job.

I might not be bigger, stronger, and faster than those guys, T conceded. Then he looked closer. *Does one of those men have drawn-in eyebrows? Does the other one have a patch of green-lightning-bolt-shaped stubble on his head?* He stood awkwardly in the middle of the all-white room as the three dark-suited men regarded him without expression. The middle man, who seemed less like an oddball than his companions, began to reach inside his jacket pocket.

Oh My God, she really is gonna get rid of me!

The middle man pulled out a tape measure.

"What's that for?" croaked T.

"We have to measure you if we're gonna get your suit ready in time," said the middle man.

★ ★ ★

Later that night, Alison, Kellyn, and Dorinda lay together in Kellyn's mom's spacious bed. But this wasn't a nostalgic reprise of the kind of fun sleepovers they used to have. They were staring intently at Alison's iPhone.

"*I never liked you. I only felt sorry for you.*"

"*I never thought you were pretty.*"

"*I hate everything about you.*"

Alison dropped the phone into the bedsheets. Watching T was too painful.

"I'm going to kill her," promised Dorinda.

"I'm doubly killing her," said Kellyn.

Alison looked at the girls lying on either side of her. "You're saying that because you've never killed anyone. If you had, you wouldn't want to do it again."

Kellyn clutched Alison's arm. "Oh My God, what if they've got married?"

"You're supposed to be making her feel better!" yelled Dorinda.

"I'm just saying. She's bananas, she loves the drama, she can have anything she wants, and she's abducted the guy of her dreams. I mean, just trying to put myself inside her head . . ."

Dorinda rolled her eyes. "That's what you'd do?"

Kellyn retorted, "That's what crazy would do. You know crazy, Dor. You know what it can make you do."

Dorinda was on the verge of exploding. Alison put her hands over both her friends' mouths. "Enough! Massively not helping. Pixie's not marrying T. You can't get married under sixteen. Unless you move to Alabama, and I don't think she's about to . . ."

And then Alison stopped talking. And then she whispered, "Oh My God."

"What?" chorused Kellyn and Dorinda.

"She's so little," breathed Alison. "She's such a brat. I always think of her as being younger than me. But she's not."

"*Get your phone out, girl*," she remembered Pixie demanding. *I need all your info.* Alison picked up her iPhone. Pixie had happily supplied all her personal details. Including date of birth. She was about to turn sixteen. "*We'll find you a molten hot guy, and you can bring him to my sweet sixteen,*" Alison remembered Pixie squealing. "*It's going to be epic, thus you need an epic date. But not too epic. He can't outshine mine. And mine's gonna be the date to end all dates, you won't even believe it.*"

"I *don't* believe it," Alison said to herself.

"*What?*" chorused Kellyn and Dorinda.

"She's not getting married," repeated Alison. But now she knew what Pixie *was* doing with T.

The following evening, the three men who had taken T's measurements returned to the all-white room to inspect their results. Once again, they regarded him without expression. Once again, T stood awkwardly as they inspected him. The dark suit hung perfectly on him. The three men looked satisfied.

Bowling Ball With Drawn-In Eyebrows Guy walked toward the white door and opened it.

The other two men gestured to T. "After you," they said.

T didn't move. "Where?"

Green Lightning Bolt Stubble Head gave T the slightest of

pushes. Not hard enough to knock him over or even off balance. Just hard enough to let T know that *if the guy wanted,* he could drop T to the ground.

T walked toward the door. "Am I going home soon? Can you at least tell me that?"

The two guys gestured to T to keep walking. T left the white room that had been his jail for the past two days. He followed the man, who walked down a dark, mahogany-lined corridor. The man stopped at a wooden door and pressed a button. The door slid open. The man indicated to T to step into the elevator.

When T and the men got out, they were on a lower level. T stared at the wood paneling and the red-velvet carpet and the imposing double doors at the end of the corridor. The three guys stood at the elevator door and looked at T.

"Go ahead," advised Green Lightning Bolt Stubble Head.

"That way?" inquired T, pointing to the big doors.

The three men all nodded yes.

T walked slowly up the corridor. He reached a hand toward the door handles. Fear of electric shock now informed his every move, so he waited a second before touching the handles. Letting out a sigh of relief, he pushed the big doors open.

Then T said, "*Oh My God!*"

THIRTY-FIVE
The Happiest Place on Earth

There was too much to take in. There was too much to see. T struggled to comprehend everything that stretched out in front of him once he'd opened the double doors. It seemed impossible that an indoor structure could house something so vast. But he saw the storefronts. And he saw the dancing fountains. And he saw the roller coaster. And the Ferris wheel. The tunnel of love. The dance floor. The pink castle that loomed in the distance. And the neon lettering that hung over it spelling out the word PIXIELAND.

Ludovic Furmanovsky had built his daughter her own theme park.

T's only experience of Pixie's mansion had been his all-white prison. The difference between that silent room and this endless assault on the senses left him disoriented. T craned his neck. Pixieland seemed to stretch up to the heavens. There was no ceiling. Instead, a computer-generated night sky was filled with impossibly twinkling stars that, when watched long enough, merged to form the words "Happy Sweet Sixteen, Pixie."

T took a few stumbling steps further inside the massive fantasy world. Pixie's name and face were everywhere. "Happy Birthday" banners hung around the perimeter. The storefronts all had names like *Pixie's Candy, Pixie's Toy Box*, and *Pixie's Hit Factory*. They all featured framed photos of the same young girl stuffing her face with candy floss, playing inside a life-size dollhouse, and singing into a microphone. Even in his frazzled, freaked-out state, T could still recognize that the little girl was Pixie. And smiling down on all the attractions in this little world that paid her homage was a ten-foot statue of the girl.

No wonder she's turned into such a needy, narcissistic nutcase, he thought. And then the lights started to go down. One by one, the storefronts went black. The lights on the Big Dipper, the roller coaster, and the tunnel of love all dimmed.

T felt the back of his neck prickle with fear. His heart started slamming in his chest. He looked up in the sky. The stars were going out. Within seconds, the gigantic theme park that had been awash in color was plunged into darkness. Except for one star. One star remained twinkling in the sea of blackness.

T looked up at it. The more he gazed, the bigger it seemed to get. And then it started falling from the sky. As the ever-expanding star fell, music began to play. It was a familiar melody. Voices took up the refrain. A choir singing the words, "Happy birthday to you, happy birthday to you, happy birthday, dear Pixie . . ."

The choir held on to the last syllable of her name long enough for a single spotlight to pick out the falling star. It was Pixie sitting inside a glittering hoop as it descended from the fake heavens.

"Happy Birthday to you," the choir ended.

Pixie extended a hand and looked straight at T.

T felt a fist shoving him forward. He found himself walking toward Pixie and reluctantly holding out a hand to help her down from the hoop. She was wearing the shimmering gold bat-wing dress. He flinched as his fingers made contact with the tendrils that curled around hers. But there was no shock.

She hugged him to her. "Thanks for coming to my birthday. This is the best present of all." Like she was overjoyed to see him. Like she hadn't kidnapped him and kept him locked in an all-white room.

The lights in the theme park went back on. For a second, T felt relief that he was not alone with Pixie. The huge space was now ringed with people. But they didn't look like they were friends. Or family. Or even members of a choir. They looked like tall, well-built professionals, just doing a job. As he scanned the impassive faces of the other party guests, T recognized the three men who had fitted him for his suit. None of the other stone-faced men had drawn-in eyebrows or green-lightning-bolt-shaped stubble, but, unknown to T, they all had something else in common. The entire population of Pixie's sweet sixteen was him and the cream of Ludovic Furmanovsky's private security force.

Pixie clapped with excitement. "I don't even know what I want to do first!" Then she scrunched her nose up at T and tittered, Yes, I do." She reached out a hand and dragged him toward the roller coaster. Before they got there, her *pixie*Phone rang.

Ludovic Furmanovsky's holographic image floated in the air. "Daddy!" she cried happily.

"Happy birthday, princess," crackled his 3-D likeness. "I wish I could have been there."

"Oh, Daddy, I'm having the most wonderful time. The boy I told you I liked? He's right here."

Ludovic Furmanovsky gave T a stern look. "You treat my little girl like the lady she is," he warned T.

You're even more insane than she is, T wanted to scream at the image. *Don't you see what's going on here?* But he was deep in the heart of enemy territory, massively outnumbered and vulnerable. So T said what he always said to overprotective fathers. "You don't have to worry about a thing, sir."

Ludovic gave T a long appraising stare. Then he said, "I don't have long. But I want to see my baby blow out her candles."

Pixie clapped and jumped up and down. The security force wheeled out a humungous heart-shaped cake. Three towering layers. Strawberry. Chocolate. Vanilla. Sixteen diamond-encrusted candles formed the flaming letter *P* in the middle of the cake. Pixie clasped her hands together and looked like she might explode from sheer happiness.

"Make a wish," said Ludovic.

"They've all come true, Daddy," she sighed. Pixie locked her eyes on T and didn't move them as she opened her mouth, took a breath, and prepared to blow. But before the first breath left her lips, the cake burst into flames. Dollops of strawberry, chocolate, and vanilla spattered over Pixie, T, and the security guys.

Pixie dropped her phone, her eyes got smaller, she clenched

her fists, and she let the rage flash across her face for half a second. Then she called out, "Hello, Kitty. Enjoying your eighth life?"

T's face lit up. *Alison!*

The Ferris wheel gondola nearest the ground creaked. The security force prepared to surround the wheel. Then they heard the footsteps. Walking calmly out into the middle of Pixieland toward the flaming cake was the girl in the red-leather jacket, the dark glasses, the black dress, and the big gold chain.

Bowling Ball With Drawn-In Eyebrows and Green Lightning Bolt Stubble Head both growled with rage. They wanted revenge so bad they could *taste* it.

Pixie let the annoyance drain from her face. Offering up a smile, she said, "What a nice surprise. I didn't think you were gonna make it. I'm afraid I can't offer you any cake. But I hope you'll have a drink."

The girl smiled back, but before she could utter a word in reply, a powerful jet of water picked her up and knocked her across the theme park, leaving her sprawled and semiconscious in the pool at the bottom of the dancing fountains.

"Alison!" T yelled in horror.

Pixie screeched in delight. "Did you think I wasn't prepared for party crashers? Did you think I wasn't prepared for *you?*" Pixie raised a thumb in the air and grinned at the two members of her security force buckling under the weight of their high-pressure water cannon. Pixie skipped up to her victim's twitching form and stood victoriously over the gasping girl.

"Awww," mocked Pixie, "you've wet yourself." She reached down to pull off her foe's big glasses, and that's when she stopped smiling. *Alison never had a nose ring before, did she? Certainly not one that infected part of her face?* Pixie stared down at the stranger in Alison's superhero costume. She stamped her foot hard and let out a bloodcurdling scream of fury and frustration. But no one heard it because the roller coaster had sprung into action. The empty cars rolled up the tracks and began to make their descent. As they did, jets of flame shot across the theme park and incinerated all the "Happy Birthday" banners. This time, Pixie's scream *was* audible. The Furmanovsky security force mounted the roller coaster and began clambering over the cars in search of the intruder.

"Up ahead!" yelled a security guy, seeing a flash of red-leather jacket.

The team charged toward the girl who was about to leap from the front car. Suddenly, a meaty paw shot out and grabbed her big gold chain, yanking her back down in her seat. Bowling Ball With Drawn-In Eyebrows grinned his wolfish grin and pulled off her dark glasses. *She didn't have this much pink glitter eye shadow on last time, did she?*

"Um . . . I'm over here," called out another girl in dark glasses and a big gold chain, this one hanging out by the storefront of Pixie's Toy Box.

Bowling Ball With Drawn-In Eyebrows looked confused.

"No, over here!" Another girl. Same costume. Somali accent.

"No, over here!"

The whispery tones of the third Hottie should have been a clue. But Pixie was consumed by irrational rage. She let out another scream. "She's had herself cloned! Daddy, I want clones!" She went to grab for her phone. But the *pixie*Phone lay on the ground melting under a chunk of blazing birthday cake. A frozen holographic image of Ludovic Furmanovsky kept repeating his last words to his daughter. *Make a wish . . . Make a wish . . . Make a wish . . .* Then the one-of-a-kind phone died and the image blipped out.

Bowling Ball with Drawn-in Eyebrows pointed an accusing finger at Pink Glitter Eye Shadow. "What's going on?"

The girl didn't get a chance to reply. The bottom of the roller coaster seemed to fall away, and she dropped out of sight.

Bowling Ball with Drawn-in Eyebrows stared down through the hole and saw Pink Glitter Eye Shadow fall into the arms of two more girls in red-leather jackets, one who seemed noticeably rotund and the other who seemed to have spent too long in the tanning booth. Bowling Ball only spent a few seconds staring down through the hole of the car, but that was enough time for a ferocious burst of flame to melt the roller-coaster tracks at the bottom of the big descent. When he looked up, Bowling Ball noticed that the car was dropping down a track that came to a sudden, jagged, melting end. With a yelp of fear, he jumped from the car.

Pixie stood by the wreckage of her cake and watched in silence as the roller-coaster car flew off the melted track and smashed into her ten-foot statue, sending it crashing to the ground. She looked at the burning "Happy Birthday" banners, the blazing storefronts, the ruined roller coaster, and the fallen statue. Then she went *bananas*!

"THIS. IS. ALL. YOUR. FAULT!" she screamed at Green Lightning Bolt Stubble Head, who was unlucky enough to be the first person in her line of fire. "YOU. RUINED. EVERYTHING!"

Once again, his first instincts were to protect his head.

A moment later, Pixie stepped over his twitching body. In the middle of her meltdown, she saw five red-jacketed girls scampering toward her big pink castle. Well, four were scampering. One was *wheeling*.

"HOW. DID. THEY. GET. IN. HERE?" shrieked Pixie.

A sixth girl in a red jacket, dark glasses, and gold chain stepped into view. "Maybe your security system's not so awesome," said the girl. "Or maybe you should treat people better." The girl pulled off her glasses.

Pixie gasped. "*Pilar?*" She stared at the maid she'd taken such innocent pleasure in torturing. "After all I've done for you?" Pixie started to point her finger at Pilar.

T shoved her. Hard. Pixie stumbled and hit the ground. She stared up at him, her face streaked with tears and hurt.

"I only wanted to share my birthday with you," she sobbed.

T knew she was done. He reached down a hand to help her up.

"So trusting," she sneered, the electricity crackling around her gold tendrils.

Then a loud pounding drumbeat echoed around the theme park. Dramatic strings sawed over the drums. Then horns began blaring. Hottie's theme. Pixie paused. T pulled his hand away. The music got louder. Pixie and T both stared in disbelief as they saw its source.

David Eels walked out into the middle of the theme park, carrying a portable iPod dock in the palm of his hand. David gave T a friendly nod. "Someone we both know once told me to write her a list of comic books and then shove it up my butt. Which is where I found *Unpopular Squad,* Volume One, Issue Five. The one where Soul Butcher looks like he's destroyed our heroes. But then everyone he's ever wronged shows up wearing superhero costumes. Forming one giant, undefeatable Unpopular Squad! And making the statement that deep down, no matter our differences, aren't we all part of a big unpopular squad? Which gave me an idea. Which then became a brilliantly choreographed plan. A plan that—"

Before David could finish, a blast of electricity smashed into the iPod dock, silencing the blaring theme.

"I don't recall inviting a dork to my birthday party," snarled Pixie, pointing a crackling finger in David's direction.

"How many times in my life am I gonna hear *that*?" He sighed.

T saw that Pixie was about to blast David. He tried to intervene. But Pixie was faster. She stabbed her finger into his arm, causing him to go numb and wince in pain. She whirled around to face David. At that moment, the neon PIXIELAND sign hanging above the big pink castle burst into flames. Pixie stared as the hundreds of lights and tubes that spelled out her name began to explode. She looked like she was about to hyperventilate. Instead, she spread her arms and rose up off the ground. Her tendriled hand lashed out in David's direction. He started running, zigzagging his way in between the shards of electricity that smashed into the ground. *Wow*, David thought as he leapt and spun and kicked his way ahead of the voltage. *Maybe I do have a dancer inside of me.*

Once she was twenty feet in the air, Pixie saw David heading toward her castle. As he made his way inside, she also saw the small red figure walking down the drawbridge. Pixie stopped rising, pointed her arms forward, and shot through the air. She passed her fallen statue and her burning banners. She didn't look down at the twisted remains of the roller coaster. Pixie kept flying until she was a few feet away from the big pink castle. It wasn't a *real* castle, of course. It was a majestic pink-stone structure whose turrets and towers spiraled toward the sky. But it was just a front. There was nothing behind the pink stone but a spiral staircase. Pixie had no recollection of this fact. As she flew closer and closer to the towers, she saw *her* castle invaded and defiled by the figure standing on the drawbridge.

"You've changed," she said to Alison.

It was true. While the saboteurs who had helped her invade Pixie's party all sported the regulation Hottie garb, Alison herself had gone for a new look. The leather jacket was replaced by a crimson Ruffian blazer. Black backpack straps were around her shoulders. The wig was gone. Her hair was now tucked under a red pilot's hat with the Hottie logo where the airline symbol would have been. The vintage Chanel shades had been returned to storage. Taking their place was a pair of white Stella McCartney wide-rim sunglasses. Beneath the jacket, she wore a short white Nike tennis skirt and her motorcycle boots.

"New costume," said Alison. Then she unbuttoned her blazer to reveal pink dog tags around her neck and a white tank top emblazoned with the burning *H*. "Same Hottie."

Pixie stared at her. "It kinda works," she admitted grudgingly.

"I was so stupid," confessed Alison. "I should have done this when I showed up that first day at *Jen*. Mix 'n' match. Little bit of the stewardess look, little bit of the Hottie . . ."

"*Shut up!*" screamed Pixie. "You ruined my birthday."

"You kidnapped my boyfriend," retorted Alison.

"He likes me better," jeered Pixie. "We totally made out, like, a hundred times."

Alison looked up at Pixie, interested. "Did he do that thing with his tongue where it's like he's spelling out the letters of the alphabet?"

"Of course." Pixie nodded smugly.

Alison gave Pixie her smuggest smile of triumph. "He never kissed you."

Pixie reddened. She balled her fists. The electricity crackled and spat between her fingers. "I'm gonna rip you apart till there's nothing left."

Looking unconcerned, Alison said, "So I suppose you don't want your present?"

Pixie's rage was superseded by her curiosity. "You got me something?"

"It would be pretty rude to show up at your party empty-handed."

Pixie snapped her sparking fingers impatiently. "What is it?"

"I'll give you a clue." Alison smiled coyly. "It starts with the same letter as your name."

"*P*?" said Pixie.

"Pee," repeated Alison.

As she said the word, the first balloon flew from the castle turret and splashed across Pixie's shimmering gold dress. Pixie's mouth opened and closed. She was beyond shock. She had no clue what was happening. The second balloon followed. Pixie screamed in disgust. "Is that *pee*?" she screeched, screwing up her face.

"Happy birthday!" said Alison.

Pixie tried to aim her tendrils at the turrets, where David, Kellyn, and Dorinda were energetically hurling pee balloons. But something was happening to her shimmering gold dress. The lights and sensors were going out. Sparks were flying from the bat wings. Pixie wasn't floating in the air anymore. Now she was *lurching* as if invisible scissors were snipping away at the wires holding her aloft.

Pixie screamed as she plummeted downward, hitting the ground with a thud.

She lay motionless for a second. Then her eyes flickered open.

"You're grounded," said Alison.

The sound of footsteps drawing closer made Alison look up. T was fighting his way through the destruction toward her. Alison broke into a run. She threw her arms around T.

"I'll never ever ever let anything bad happen to you ever again," she gasped, clinging to him.

As they hugged, David, Kellyn, Dorinda, the former PBG, and the ex-*Jen* staffers all ran down the drawbridge.

"That? . . ." began David.

". . . was *classic*!" completed Kellyn.

David and Kellyn ran to embrace Alison and T. The PBG/ Dorinda Militia, Pilar, and the ex-*Jen* girls hugged each other. Kellyn glanced up from the clinch to see Dorinda standing by herself, looking lost. The girls opened their circle to include her in the shrieky group hug. But Kellyn couldn't stop thinking how alone her friend seemed. T smiled and hugged everybody, but Alison could see he was exhausted, the strain of the last couple of days written over his face. She squeezed T's hand, and they started to walk away from the castle. As she did, one of the "Happy Birthday" banners that was burning around the perimeter of Pixieland floated down to the ground. Alison found herself gazing up toward the roof. Now that the banner had fallen, she could see what was underneath: the words "Happy Sixth Birthday, Pixie." With a sinking feeling, Alison remembered what had made her decide to bond with Pixie.

"Is it just you and your dad, Pixie?"

"Since I was six. Just before my birthday."

Ten years ago. Since the birthday party she never got to have. Ten years of waiting to find someone who lived up to her impossible standards. Ten years of being completely indulged and, at the same time, completely ignored by her father. Alison sighed. Pixie was so completely hateable, but she couldn't completely hate her.

"Wait a minute," Alison told T. "I can't leave her like this." Alison walked back to Pixie, who was curled up in a fetal ball. "Pixie?" she said softly.

The girl stared into the fake heavens, her eyes two little bullets of loathing.

"I'm gonna say something to you, and then I'll leave you alone."

Pixie showed no sign of being aware Alison was speaking.

Alison gestured to her group of friends, who were standing nearby. "All these people have let me down or fought with me or stabbed me in the back or tried to *bludgeon* me at one time or another."

Kellyn yawned loudly. She *hated* the superhero morality speech.

"One of them's doing it right now," said Alison, her voice rising in annoyance. "But they're all here right now when I need them. Because that's what friends do. They accept each other's flaws and failings. They bitch and they bicker, but when it matters, they've got your back. You need to give someone a chance to do that for you, Pixie. You can't keep throwing yourself at people and then dropping them the second they do something to displease you. Otherwise, you'll be all alone. You won't even have your daddy."

Pixie continued staring into the sky.

"I wasn't kidding about the birthday present," Alison went on. "I really did bring you something." Alison pulled off her backpack. Young Angus's head poked out. She put the bag on the ground and unzipped it all the way. The Maltipoo was dressed in a tiny doggie schoolboy uniform, just like the one worn by AC/DC's guitarist, Angus Young.

"I brought you a friend. Try and keep him." Alison carried the dog over to Pixie.

"Go back to Mommy," she whispered.

Then she turned and walked back to her friends, all of whom were staring at her with amazement.

"After what she did to T. What she did to you? You were that nice and forgiving?" said Kellyn.

Alison shrugged. "I wasn't that nice. I gave Young Angus a bowlful of Fiji water before the mission. She's got some more pee headed her way."

The rescue party made its way to the driveway of the Furmanovsky mansion, where Designated Dean was waiting in the Hottiemobile. He honked the horn impatiently. But the big guy's cholesterol-riddled plus-size heart had been revealed. Everyone in the Department of Hotness knew his honks were expressions of relief and celebration. Alison kept her hand around T's. David and Kellyn had their arms wrapped around each other's waists. Amandine, Cutesy Woo, Elspeth, and Waris babbled happily about the way they'd been freed from the grip of their oppressor.

"Way to stick it to the boss!" called out Alison. The *Jen* staffers grinned at her. The PBG/Dorinda Militia moved in a tight, excited, chattering circle. Alison looked back at them. "You girls? Can I just say, 'Awesome, *awesome* job'? You're completely rehabilitated. Dor, you should be very proud of your crew."

Dorinda brought up the rear. She didn't have her arms around anyone.

Once again, Kellyn looked back and saw her old friend standing alone. She bit her lip. What was it she'd said to Designated Dean? *Weird when that happens, huh? When you find yourself caring?* Kellyn looked at David. "Give me a minute," she said. "I just need to talk to—"

She didn't get a chance to finish her sentence. Suddenly, all anyone could hear was screaming. The Um Girl's hair was on fire.

THIRTY-SIX
Powerless

The Um Girl's shrieking friends threw coats over her head. But even as they rushed to extinguish the flames that had erupted from her hair, bolts of electricity were raining down from the night sky. Alison and T dived forward to pull the screaming, terrified girls to the safety of the Hottiemobile. Before they could reach them, a blast of electricity smashed straight into T, knocking him across the driveway and leaving him twitching on the ground. Alison yelled out in horror. Then she looked up and her jaw dropped.

Pixie was standing on top of her balcony, her golden bat wings spread, electricity flying from her tendrils. Alison shuddered in fear. Pixie looked like a gargoyle come to life.

"DID YOU REALLY THINK MY DADDY WOULDN'T

GIVE ME A BACKUP UNIT? I JUST NEEDED A MINUTE TO RECHARGE MY BATTERIES. NOW I'M EVEN MORE POWERFUL!"

Pixie swooped down from the balcony and headed straight for the Hottiemobile, just as David was helping Kellyn inside. She shot a jet of electricity at David, causing him to scream in pain. Pixie let out a mocking imitation of David's terrified reaction, then she fired at Elspeth, knocking her wheelchair over on its side. Amandine ran to help her fallen friend and received another burst of electricity, which left her convulsing on the ground.

Alison threw herself in front of her friends and fired two blasts of flame at Pixie. She brushed them off like they were snowflakes. *The pee was useless*, thought Alison miserably.

Pixie hovered in the air, smiling down at Alison. "Thanks so much for the lecture on friendship," she said, her voice dripping sarcasm. "It spoke to me in a very real way. In fact, it affected me so much I'm going to let all your friends go. I'm not going to touch a hair on any of their heads. Well, apart from the hair that's on fire. Can't undo that. So what do you say, Allywally? Your precious friends get to go on with their very important lives?"

Alison knew that this was headed somewhere bad. But she cautiously nodded her assent.

"And you sacrifice yourself for them."

Welcome to somewhere bad! "Pixie . . ." began Alison.

"Oh, what? America's No. 1 *Jen* Girl turns out to be a filthy, lying hypocritic? Or maybe, just maybe, she's being real. Maybe she's more like me than she wants to admit."

"I *am* like you, Pixie," shouted Alison. "We've got so much in common. That's why I know I can help you."

Pixie shot a bolt of electricity in T and Dorinda's direction. Alison screamed out in fear.

"Tell the truth," yelled Pixie, "you wouldn't sacrifice yourself for them because it would be a waste. You're special. They're not."

Alison shook her head. "You don't have any friends, so you don't know. Every one of these people is special to me."

Pixie laughed coldly. "Cutesy Woo's special? Wheels is special? The gap-toothed Somali is special?"

Alison nodded, her eyes shining with sincerity. "Every one of them."

"Prove it," sneered Pixie. She waggled her fingers. "Take a few volts and your little geek buddy lives to fight another day."

Alison looked over at the Hottiemobile. Kellyn was crying and clinging to a dazed David.

Alison gritted her teeth and walked toward Pixie. "Hit me," said Alison.

Pixie grinned and shot electricity into Alison's body. Alison howled in pain and dropped to her knees.

"Wow, Allywally. Impressed. Now, how about the geek's bitchy girlfriend? She's not worth anything to you. I know the type. Undermines you to your face. Tries to puncture your self-esteem. You ought to thank me for blowing her to bits."

Alison pushed herself to her feet. With an effort, she faced Pixie. Her eyes were clear. "Hit me again," she commanded.

Pixie smiled. "You're an example to us all. A *glowing* example." She pointed her tendrils at Alison.

"NO!" screamed Kellyn. "Don't hurt her!"

Pixie cupped a hand to her ear. "What was that? Hurt her?" She fired at Alison.

T, Kellyn, Dorinda, David, and all the girls cried out in horror. Alison lay motionless on the ground.

"Best birthday ever," said Pixie happily. She gazed down at the quaking, sobbing group beneath her. "I wish I could do this all night. But I don't think Allywally's got much life left in her."

Alison let out a gasp of pain.

"You *go*, girl!" yelped Pixie. "Seriously, though, sweetie, I've got enough juice to keep Las Vegas lit up. But you . . . let's just say your candle's about to go out. I'm gonna make it easy on you. One last party game. You soak up one final shock from me, and I let T go free. And, let's face it, it's *me* that's making the bigger sacrifice here."

"Alison, no," gasped T. He tried to pull himself to his feet.

Alison pushed a hand into the dirt and dragged herself upright. She could barely see straight. But she managed to get to her feet.

"It doesn't have to be like this, Alison," said Pixie, turning sincere. "Say the word, this all stops. I fry a couple of your little clone girls. Pink slip the rest of my traitorous staff. We all go home happy."

Alison struggled to speak. "You'll never be happy," she managed to croak.

"I'm happy right now." Pixie fired one last blast of electricity into Alison and watched as she fell into the dirt. "Wow," she gasped at Alison's stunned, sobbing group of friends, "She really did like you. You must be an awesome group. Maybe I should try to get to know you all. But then, you ruined my birthday party. And you're trespassing on my property. I'm quite within my rights to defend myself against a gang of intruders . . ."

She fired a few stray volts at the ground. Everyone screamed in terror. Pixie let out a loud cheerful laugh. She was having the *best* time!

Alison couldn't move. She couldn't open her eyes. Her head was filled with the smell of burning. *All that's left of me is a few scattered thoughts. I'm not going to make it . . . What's that touching my face? Why is it so wet?* With an effort, Alison managed to force open an eye. Another eye was close to hers. It was Young Angus. He was rubbing his wet nose against her cheek and licking her. Alison let out a moan of recognition. Then she saw that the dog had brought her something. Something glittering and round with a familiar burning *H* at its center.

Pixie flew toward T. "You didn't really think you were getting away from me that easily, did you?"

Dorinda went to push herself in front of him.

"Please," laughed Pixie. "You think you can stop me from getting what I want? *No one can!*"

"I can, " said Alison.

Pixie stopped and looked around. Alison hadn't made it to her feet. But she was facing upward and her eyes were open. Pixie looked both impressed and frustrated. She swooped toward Alison, her tendrils crackling. As Pixie drew closer, Alison grabbed the yo-yo Young Angus had brought her. She summoned up every last bit of strength and lashed it out as hard as she could. The wire lit up. The steel ball caught fire and made contact with the tip of Pixie's finger seconds before her electricity was unleashed.

"You *burned* me!" gasped Pixie. She put her scalded fingers in her mouth. Electricity flooded through her body. For a second, she shone like an angel. Then she screamed, "*Daddeeee!*" dropped from the sky, and lay in a motionless, smoking heap in the dirt.

"*Now* you're grounded," said Alison.

THIRTY-SEVEN
Sympathy for the Devil

Meet Ally: America's NO. 1
JEN GIRL BLOGS FOR U!

Oh My God, you GUYS!!!! I can't believe my time at Jen is up already. I learned so much and met so many amazzzing people I'll NEVER forget. But things r changing at Jen. My awesome friends Amandine, Elspeth, Waris, and Cutesy Woo are getting together 2 take the rains (sp?). I wish I could have stayed longer, but I got so much out of my time on the 2wenty-3hird floor. Summer's just around the corner, and I'm looking forward 2 spending every minute with my friends and especially w/ my #1 Cute Guy BF. But no matter what I do in life, I'll never forget those few amazzzing months when I was . . . America's No. 1 Jen Girl.

Xxxxxx,

A

P.S.: One of my firstest and bestest Jen frenz ☺ has to spend most of the summer in the hospital :(. Sux for her, but if you ever had fun reading the What's Hot and What's Not List, then why not send a Get Well card to the girl behind it. Her name's Pixie Furmanovsky, and she's in the Schute-Bruggeman clinic in Beverly Hills (she's soooo lucky—all the stars go there!!). She won't be able 2 write back or talk 2 u (she can't even eat on her own. Ewwww!), but it'll mean a lot 2 her 2 know she's got some friends out there . . .

(Monday, May 22, 2:30 p.m.)

Pixie's private ward was filled with letters and cards, balloons, flowers, and candy. Alison felt a brief burst of pride in her final *Jen* blog. But as she stood out in the corridor of the clinic, where she accidentally had received her powers, Alison looked at the girl lying motionless in her bed. Pixie had received the best medical care billions of dollars could buy. She was off life support. She was able to swallow spoonfuls of food. She was no longer bandaged from head to toe.

But even from her vantage point outside the room, it was clear to Alison that Pixie hadn't really come back to life. She was staring up at the ceiling, her face blank, her eyes dead, her body devoid of movement. *She's still alone*, thought Alison sadly. *I should come and visit her every day. I should show her that I'm here for her. And that way she'll become a better person. Oh God, I really don't want to visit her every day . . .*

Alison's inner dialogue was interrupted by a brusque male voice echoing from further down the corridor. The voice talked about cutbacks and buyouts and mergers, and then it screamed with pain. Pixie's father, Ludovic Furmanovsky, pulled his tiny, melting Bluetooth from his ear. He was so wrapped up in holding a handkerchief over his wounded ear, he didn't see Alison standing a few feet away from him.

"Hello, Mr. Furmanovsky," she finally said.

Ludovic Furmanovsky gave her a vague glance.

"Nice to see you again," she continued. His interest flickered and began to die. Then she held out a hand. "Cole," she said briskly. "Dr. Alison Cole."

Suddenly, she had his attention. The billionaire looked her up and down. "You're not a doctor," he said.

"And you're not a father," she replied, taking hold of Ludovic's outstretched hand. He winced in pain. She pulled him closer. "You made Pixie into a crazy psycho nut. Now you need to unmake her." Ludovic Furmanovsky squirmed under the heat from Alison's hand. She did not relax her grip. "I want you to be worried about what time she comes home. I want you to disapprove of whoever she's got a crush on. I want you to hate what she wears. I want you to be a Helicopter Dad."

Ludovic Furmanovsky gasped. "What's a Helicopter Dad?"

"Always hovering," replied Alison. Then she pulled her hand away. The tycoon exhaled in shock and stared at his tender hand.

Alison kept her eyes on him. "I want you here every day. I want her sick of you."

Ludovic Furmanovsky was about to call for help. Then he found himself looking into his daughter's room. Once he saw the blank expression on Pixie's face, he suddenly realized he could fill the entire hospital with flowers, candy, and balloons, but he still wasn't giving her the one thing she needed. The protest died in his throat. "I'll do it," he said quietly. "I'll be here. Every day. I'll give her whatever she wants. I'll give her the world."

"You already gave her the world," said Alison, "and she broke it. Just be there when she needs you. Just make her feel loved."

Ludovic Furmanovsky nodded and made his way into Pixie's room. As he walked away from Alison, he murmured, "Thank you, Doctor. . . ."

Alison remained standing in the corridor until she saw Ludovic kiss his daughter on her forehead. Then he sat by the bed and began opening the piles of letters and cards from *Jen* readers. When he started reading to her, Alison knew her work was done. She turned away from the window, a smile on her face.

"Doctor," she said to herself, delighted.

THIRTY-EIGHT
Everybody Hurts

Two weeks had gone by since the eventful climax of Pixie's sweet sixteen. Two weeks and Alison hadn't heard a word from T. She knew he was shaken up during the ride home from Pixie's mansion. She'd held on to his hand and told him everything was all right. But he'd stared out the window of the Hottiemobile the whole way back to Los Feliz. He hadn't wanted her to come home with him, either. So Alison gave him his distance. She understood. Everyone was traumatized. Everyone had emerged from that mish with their own particular set of battle scars.

But then two days turned into three, and then a week had gone by without a call or an email or a text. Eventually, Alison turned up on T's doorstep. The lovely Birgit was back from Japan.

She was *so* sorry, but T didn't want to see anyone. Which gave Alison the chance to say, "*I'm* not 'anyone.'"

Birgit, however, was rigid. Her stepson was feeling exhausted and withdrawn. He needed to recharge his batteries. And now two weeks had gone by. Kellyn, Dorinda, David, and even The Um Girl were all back at school, and none of them seemed the worse for wear. The Um Girl had even stopped wearing her trademark Burberry bucket hat so she could proudly show off her shaved head.

Alison's fears of the nonconfrontational dumping began to reassert themselves. So she skipped out early from school and took a cab to Los Feliz. Where she saw the IN ESCROW sign on T's lawn. And then she saw T loading travel luggage into the trunk of a Town Car.

Alison climbed out of the taxi and walked toward him. T didn't look surprised to see her. Neither did he look particularly pleased. This would have been the most perfect opportunity for Alison to throw a colossal tantrum. But she knew T had been through hell. So she waited by the Town Car, giving him the chance to prepare what he wanted to say.

"My dad took the Sony offer," T began in a flat voice.

Alison broke in, "That was Pixie! She set that whole thing up to get you alone."

"It was a real offer, Alison. They want him to work out there. And he wants his family with him."

Alison hadn't expected this. "And you want to go?"

T loaded another case into the trunk.

"But you'll miss school. You'll miss being president. You'll miss your friends."

She stared hard at T. *Say, "I'll miss you." This is your cue. Just say it. It'll make us both feel better.*

T slammed the trunk shut. Alison inhaled sharply. A horrible, *inconceivable* thought had just occurred to her. "Are you going so you can get away from me?"

T approached Alison. He circled his hands around her wrists. The blank expression started to leave his face. She could see he wanted to tell her what he was feeling.

"*What?*" she urged.

"Pixie," he finally said. "That night."

"It's over," she said firmly.

"*That's* over. But that won't be the worst thing that ever happens to you."

Alison saw the pain in his eyes. "But we've got each other. And I'll always protect you, you know that."

T let his hands fall away from Alison's wrists. "See, I should be saying that to you."

Alison shot him a disbelieving look. "What does it matter who says it as long as we both mean it? I know you'll always be there for me just like I'll always be here for you *if you'll let me.*"

T stared at the ground. "It's just . . . I see your life. The only part I see in it for me is being scared for you and being worried for you. Worried that this is the one where you don't come out alive."

Alison rubbed at her eyes. *Don't cry*, she warned herself. "Okay, I get it," she said with as much good cheer as she could muster. "Change of scene. Change of pace. New Pocky flavors. And it's a small world. We can Skype every day. I'll come visit.

And it won't be forever. So why don't we just say that this is *sayonora*?"

T gave her a sad, regretful look in return. "No, I think this is goodbye."

Alison found herself looking back over the past few weeks. She'd received countless electric shocks. She'd been kicked in the face and dropped down an elevator shaft. None of these assaults hurt worse than the six words T had just uttered.

"I could make you stay," she found herself whispering, even though she knew these were not the words she wanted to say. "I could burn your luggage and all your clothes. I could burn your passport. They wouldn't let you on the plane. They'd send you home."

"Alison . . ." T said quietly, trying to stop her. But she couldn't stop.

"I could burn the plane. Then you'd have to stay."

Every wrong word she said looked like it made T more uncomfortable and more eager to get away from her. "But that's what you hate about me, isn't it? That I'm such a freak of nature I could even think about burning down an airport."

T raised his eyebrows. "An airport? A minute ago, it was just a plane."

She reached out a hand and began to pull the zipper of his sweatshirt up and down. "I'm raising the stakes all the time. I'll take down a blimp if that gets you to stay."

T looked impressed. "I'm worth an entire blimp?"

Alison let herself smile. He was being playful. She still had a shot. "You are worth an entire blimp to me," she repeated with utmost gravity.

He covered the hand that was still clutching his zipper. "Can you do me a favor? Can you never call yourself a freak of nature again?" T's eyes grew more intense and his voice got lower. *This is good*, thought Alison. "You saved my life.," T continued. "You saved your father's life. You saved all your friends. You're an amazing girl and you're my hero."

Yessss, exulted Alison. *Tokyo can suck it. He's staying right here.*

"But . . ."

There's a but? . . .

T looked at her sadly. "I'm not a hero. I'm just a guy."

Alison felt herself choking up. "You're more than that to me. You're everything to me."

T winced. "Why do you have to be so beautiful? Why do you have to be so adorable?"

"I don't know!" moaned Alison, caught halfway between laughter and tears. "I picked the short straw."

They both found themselves smiling. The smiles led to a kiss. While they were kissing, Alison thought, *I could make this moment last forever. If I really really try, I could do it.*

But the kiss ended. And that was it. He wanted to go. Even though she could tell from the tears forming at the corners of his eyes and the way he wrapped his arms around her and held her tight that he really *didn't*.

And then he was gone. Alison stood in the street, watching the Town Car dwindle into the distance. But she didn't cry. She didn't run after the car. She didn't scream his name. But she wasn't made of stone. Anyone who knew her circumstances could have forgiven Alison for stretching out a hand and setting the IN ESCROW sign alight.

* * *

At that exact moment, David was browsing through the new releases at Meltdown Comics on Sunset when his phone vibrated.

"About time," he muttered.

He and Kellyn had made a pact to each try and appreciate the other's tastes. He agreed to go shopping with her on Melrose Avenue if she put in her time digging through comics at Meltdown. But she was over twenty minutes late, and he was pretty sure she was calling him with a hastily constructed lie. He pulled out his black RAZR and read the text.

"Yr finger's healed so my charity work's done. Don't call me or try 2 talk. Lets just act like this never happened. K"

David stared at the text so long the words began to blur. He went to call Kellyn. Then his mind began conjuring up worst-case scenarios. It wasn't much fun reading those words, but how much more painful would it be to hear them? And, as he knew, Kellyn would have no problem plunging her rusty dagger into his gaping wound of a heart.

But why would she? Why now? he wondered. *You* know *her. She's not mean, not really.* And then David remembered his doomed crush on Alison and how much it hurt when she rejected him. *Why not now?* He nodded to himself. *It was always gonna happen. A guy like you doesn't get to be with a girl like that. Welcome back to real life, Dork.*

David went to leave Meltdown. As he approached the front door, a chorus of voices yelled, "Eels!" It was Phlegmy, Tiny Head, Toenail, and Odor Eater. Of course. New comics day.

And then a voice said, "Um . . . does this place sell frozen yogurt?"

Phlegmy, Tiny Head, Toenail, and Odor Eater were unexpectedly accompanied by The Um Girl, Infected Nose Ring, Too Long In The Tanning Booth, and Pink Glitter Eye Shadow.

Noting the bewilderment clouding David's features, Tiny Head announced, "The ladies here expressed an interest in immersing themselves in the culture of the superhero."

The Um Girl gave David a knowing look. "Um . . . yeah," she said. "We all wanted to find out more since *that night* when *that thing* happened."

Odor Eater ignored her heavy-handed conversational hints. "And, of course, we were only too happy to act as ambassadors. To lead these charming novices down the dimly lit labyrinth of the fantastic." So saying, Odor Eater emitted a theatrical yawn and then casually attempted to drape his arm around Infected Nose Ring's shoulders. The horrified expression on her face might have been amusing to David if he hadn't been dying inside.

"Hang out, Eels," invited Phlegmy. "You can introduce our new friends to the Punisher."

"And then you can show them some comic books," broke in Toenail.

Phlegmy burst into fits of laughter, which rapidly developed into racking coughs. The former PBG looked on in stony silence.

"Another time," said David, hurrying out of the store, phlegm-filled coughs echoing in his ears.

Out on Sunset, David walked quickly toward the nearest bus stop.

"Um . . . David Eels?"

David looked around. The Um Girl had followed him out on

the street. She looked a little like Tank Girl with her tiny tufts of hair.

"Um . . . are you okay?"

"I'm fine," said David. "Just a little salmonella poisoning."

"I'm so glad we're friends again," Dorinda iChatted to Kellyn later that night. "I didn't know how much I was going to miss having someone to talk to."

Kellyn sat in her bedroom and looked at her friend's lovely face. "But you had a whole crew of followers. They hung on your every word. You were like Oprah. You were Doprah."

Dorinda laughed. "I don't think I'm cut out to be a cult leader."

Kellyn nodded, happy she had initiated their nightly pre-bed chat sessions. She wanted to rebuild her friendship with Dorinda, but she wanted her to know that this time was going to be different. This time Kellyn would listen. She'd make sure Dorinda never felt alone or invisible again. She wasn't capable of the kind of sacrifice that Alison had been prepared to make to save her friends. But there was something Kellyn could do for Dorinda. She leaned closer to the screen. "Listen, Dor, there's something I need to tell you."

Dorinda interrupted, "There's something I need to tell you, too . . ."

Kellyn quelled her irritation. *Rebuilding the friendship*, she told herself. *Learning to listen.* She made a *"Go ahead"* gesture at the screen.

Dorinda's eyes darted around as if she were checking for interlopers. She moved closer to the camera and lowered her voice to a whisper. "I really like T," she said. Before Kellyn could react, Dorinda blurted out, "I would never *ever* do anything about it. Not while he's with Alison. But we hung out a few weeks ago, and we totally connected, and I know he felt it, too. Sometimes you just know. You've heard the way Alison talks about him. I get the feeling she's ready to move on. But I wouldn't just swoop in there like some sort of vulture. I'd totally wait until she's found someone else, which should take about eight seconds. You can *never* tell her. Promise?"

"T? You like T?" said Kellyn, surprised. And then she thought, *I'm about to drop dead.* Kellyn had no other explanation for the complicated and horrible series of reactions she was suddenly experiencing. She felt nauseous. She felt dizzy. She felt like she was about to faint. She felt an incredible sense of loss. But Kellyn knew she could not show any of the things she felt. Not if she wanted to keep her friend. Banishing the faintest trace of emotion from her face, she touched a hand to her heart. "It's in the steely vault. You can tell me *anything*," she swore. "And I'll always listen."

Dorinda yawned and made an apologetic face. "I'm so glad we're friends again," she repeated.

Then she signed off.

Kellyn sat in stunned silence for a second before putting her computer to sleep. Despite her best intentions, it was only now that it had finally hit home why she should have paid more attention to Dorinda in the past. If she'd listened, she'd have understood that Dorinda fell in love *a lot*. If Kellyn had known that, she might not have made what she now realized was a terrible mistake. She might not have sent a text that she didn't think she could ever take back.

With these thoughts rattling around in her head, Kellyn lay down on her bed. She reached under her pillow and pulled out David's Jesus and Mary Chain T-shirt. Then Kellyn buried her face in it and cried herself to sleep.

THIRTY-NINE

*The Legendary Adventures of the
Department of Heartbreak*

Roger Cole returned home after a long day's work. He was in a good mood. The endless case against British Airways looked like it was going to end up settled out of court and in his favor. His relationship with Alison was steadily improving. They were going to have a thing to do together. No more burying himself in work. Now he couldn't wait to get home and spend time with Alison. It was going to feel great to laugh with her again. He wandered into his kitchen to find his daughter eating a bowl of Wheaties.

"Cereal for dinner?" He grinned and ruffled Alison's hair. "Is that what all the cool kids are doing now?"

In a split second, Alison changed from placid Wheaties-munching to a beacon of blazing fury. She jumped to her feet, sending the kitchen stool flying behind her, where it landed with a thud on the floor.

Roger took a step back, shocked by Alison's scarlet face and angry eyes. Before he could say anything, she started bawling at him.

"LEAVE ME ALONE! I CAN'T BREATHE IN HERE. ALL I GET IS QUESTIONS, QUESTIONS, QUESTIONS. WHERE ARE YOU GOING? WHAT ARE YOU DOING? WHO WERE YOU TALKING TO? I CAN'T TAKE IT ANYMORE. . . ." Alison paused for breath.

Roger stared at her, shocked and concerned. "What is it, Alison?" he asked. "What's happened?"

In a voice that could shatter glass, she screeched, "WHAT'S MY FACEBOOK STATUS?"

Roger groped for a reply. Too late.

"ALISON WANTS TO BE ALONE!" she yelled, rushing from the kitchen and charging up to her room.

Roger remained frozen to the spot for another moment until the sound of Alison's bedroom door slamming shut brought him back to life.

This is my life from now on: Wheaties, screaming, and weeping, thought Alison as she attempted to repair the damage done to her face by fifteen minutes of uninterrupted crying. But then, she reflected, she'd felt equally devastated when her first boyfriend, Warren what-did-I-*ever*-see-in-him Douglas, dumped her. It had seemed like a tragedy at the time. But now she could barely remember what he looked like. Because he'd been so comprehensively replaced by T Who had also dumped her. *So even though I feel horrible just now, I can console myself with the thought that I'll meet someone else.* Alison let her thought play out to its logical conclusion. *Someone who'll end up dumping me.* Alison staggered from her dresser and let herself fall facedown on her bed. Two more minutes of industrial-strength wailing followed. Then she sat up, wiped her streaming eyes and nose, and switched on the TV. *Show me something shallow and stupid,* she begged. *Something I can just switch my brain off and stare at. Something that won't remind me of how miserable and lonely I am.*

Alison flipped channels idly. Shallow and stupid were everywhere, but she couldn't focus. Her remote-control finger grazed through the grid, stopping at the premium channels. Almost every movie showing was something she'd sat and watched with T Every movie she passed brought back memories, tastes, and smells. She could feel his presence in the room. Alison stopped flipping at the station showing the Pixar cartoon *Wall-E*. They'd never seen this. It was a kiddie movie. She could switch her brain off and stare blankly.

After a few moments, Alison was howling even louder. *When EVE, the cute robot, set things on fire with her laser-blaster fingers, Wall-E didn't freak out and run off to Japan with his family. He loved her more. He stowed away on a starship so he could be near her.* And that's when the front door buzzed.

"T!" gasped Alison. It had to be. It was too perfect. It was a movie ending. Alison flew from her bed, pausing only to dab a tissue at her eyes. Then she hurtled downstairs, heading her father off as he made his way to the door. Roger, who had earlier that evening been confronted by a raging inferno, now found himself squinting from the huge beaming grin that was radiating from his daughter.

"Go about your business, old man," she told him happily. "I got this."

Roger shook his head, confused. Alison watched him go and then inhaled. Calming herself and preparing for an explosion of happiness, she opened the door.

"I got dumped," said David.

Alison felt herself deflate. But misery loves company. So she said, "I got dumped, too."

"I got dumped by text."

"I got dumped by fleeing the country." Alison gestured for David to follow her to the kitchen. "You're gonna need Wheaties," she assured him.

Even though she was consumed by her own pain and heartache, Alison possessed enough empathy to feel outraged on David's behalf as she listened to the sad story of Kellyn's text treachery.

"You could have had Dorinda. She's sweet and nice, and she does voices and card tricks, and she cooks, and then there's the whole boob thing. But, no, you had to take the journey into the heart of darkness."

Alison lay on her bed staring up at the ceiling. David remained on the floor. Their collective unhappiness filled the room. Then the front door buzzed again. Alison couldn't stop herself. She bounced straight off her bed and shot out the door.

T! she thought as she raced downstairs. *This time. The perfect movie fake out. I wanted it to be him so badly last time that it couldn't be him. This time.*

Once again, Roger headed for the door. Once again, Alison banished him back to the bowels of the house. Once again, she calmed herself, breathed in, pushed her hair back behind her ears, and opened the door.

"I'm never doing a good thing ever again." Kellyn scowled, pushing past Alison and stomping sulkily into hallway toward the stairs.

"Wowza!" was all Alison could say. She'd managed to divert Kellyn away from her bedroom and out to the pool. Her disappointment at the continuing lack of T at her front door was huge and painful. But it was ever so slightly lessened by her astonishment at the story Kellyn poured out. A story of friendship, sacrifice, and misunderstanding.

"You gave away a boy," marveled Alison, "a whole boy?"

"I know!" said a pained Kellyn. "Don't let anyone ever try to tell you it's better to give than to receive. Total lie."

"You can get him back, though," Alison said.

Kellyn shook her head emphatically. "I can never see him again. I would rather die. In fact, I'd rather *he* die. And Dorinda has to die, too. I can never look at her again. Whoever it is, someone's got to die. Otherwise, I'll just be constantly reminded that I'm as weak and stupid as everyone else."

Alison's phone vibrated. *T? This time?* She gave it a quick hopeful glance. No T. Dorinda. The text read, "Need 2 talk. I'll be over in 60 secs."

Does nobody respect my Facebook status? wondered Alison, bitterly.

Ten minutes later, Alison had snuck a confused Dorinda into the guesthouse and was patiently listening to an outpouring of guilt about a secret relationship that was entirely imaginary.

"I would never, ever want to hurt you for the world. Neither would T," insisted Dorinda in a quavery voice. "We both love you *so* much. That's what makes this so awful."

Alison retained a placid expression as she listened to her friend babble. She'd been shocked, moments earlier, when Kellyn told her about Dorinda's secret love for T. But now, as she sat in the guesthouse and half listened to apologies and explanations fly out of Dorinda's mouth, she was bleakly amused. This, after all, was someone whose imagination was so overactive she'd created and maintained a credible French identity for three consecutive years. It was no stretch for her to seize on the seed of friendship offered by T and in the space of a few days allow it to blossom into a thrilling, forbidden romance. Alison let Dorinda yammer on for a few more minutes before interrupting her with a curt, "He's moved to Japan."

Dorinda responded in the only possible way. "IT'S ALL MY FAULT!" she sobbed.

Alison was on the verge of setting her straight. Then they both heard the howl of pain coming from inside the house.

Bored by Alison's absence, Kellyn had wandered into the Cole house and made her way up to Alison's bedroom for the purposes of snooping and pilfering. Her head was full of anticipation about what she might uncover in Alison's bedroom. She didn't expect to push open the door and see David sitting on the floor eating a bowl of Wheaties and flipping TV channels.

"Where've you been?" said David, without looking around. The lack of response caused him to shift his gaze from the screen. Standing in the doorway was the girl who had, only a day ago, dumped him by text.

The next twenty seconds were the longest and most uncomfortable in Kellyn's life. She felt her face flush crimson. She could feel her heart beating in triple time. Her *hair* was tingling. She wanted to turn and run, but none of her limbs seemed to be working. She wanted to say *something*. But she'd lost the ability to make sounds come out of her mouth. Most of all, she wanted David to know she was sorry. But she was physically incapable of saying sorry. So she did the only thing she could. She took a step back toward the door. Then she held out her hand, squeezed her eyes shut, and kicked the door so that it slammed on her pinky.

We might well be the most pathetic group of people on the planet, thought Alison as she surveyed the sad cast of characters assembled in awkward silence around her bedroom. Kellyn with her bruised, bandaged pinky. Dorinda mourning the demise of an entirely imaginary relationship. David who was starting to feel like a pawn in a game he didn't understand. *And me*, she thought. *The leader of the losers. The most pitiful of them all. Queen of the magical land of Pathetica.*

It was clear from the lack of conversation and the strenuous attempt to avoid meeting each other's eyes that everyone in the room harbored similar self-pitying sentiments. They all fixated on the TV screen. When Kellyn had made her surprise appearance in the bedroom, David's channel flipping had frozen on the local news. The four of them were now staring dully at stories of runaway pets and traffic congestion. As the reporter on-screen talked about how upcoming roadwork would affect the next morning's commute, the occupants of Alison's bedroom gradually found their attention being captured by the scene going on *behind* the reporter. He may have been delivering his report clad in a sober gray suit, but there was a riot of color in the background. Orange, to be exact.

As the reporter droned on, a group of young people in bright orange jumpsuits were picking up garbage from the shoulder of the freeway. And the more they focused on the juvenile offenders, the more one particular orange-suited individual started to stand out from the rest of the crowd.

"Am I losing my mind or is that Treasure Spinney?" asked Kellyn.

"Oh My God!" exclaimed Dorinda. "It *is*!"

"She's a juvenile offender!" shouted David. "Her acting was literally criminal!"

And suddenly, the awkwardness was gone. The silence evaporated. The room was filled with laughter. It was laughter at someone else's misfortune, but it was still the best any of them had felt all night. *Almost all of them.* While David, Kellyn, and Dorinda grew increasingly hysterical over the sad fate of America's former favorite TV star, Alison stayed silent. She couldn't join her friends in crowing over Treasure's demise. *I feel guilty*, she thought sadly. *How pathetic is that?*

FORTY

We Can Be Heroes

The morning after Treasure Spinney made her unexpected return to network television, the members of the Department of Hotness squeezed into the Hottiemobile and went on a road trip. As Designated Dean drove down the 101 freeway, Alison kept her eyes peeled for a telltale flash of orange.

Finally, she saw what she was looking for. A group of jump-suit-clad juvenile offenders were listlessly picking trash from the side of the freeway. And one of the group, a girl the size of a linebacker, was looking to pick a fight with a much smaller opponent.

"Pull over," said Alison.

★ ★ ★

"You think you're better than me 'cuz you were on TV. Well, you ain't on TV now, *Sunday Mundy*. You're picking up trash on the highway," the linebacker-size trash picker was saying to Treasure Spinney.

Treasure said nothing. She kept her eyes on the ground. When she bent down to pick up a flattened Coke can, the linebacker chick gave Treasure a sudden shove. She fell backward, landing on her butt. On the edge of the freeway. Where every passing car could see her.

"You gonna cry now?" mocked the linebacker chick.

And then something unexpected happened. Rips began appearing in the linebacker chick's jumpsuit. First the arms slid off. Then the legs concertina'd down to her ankles. The remaining material was quickly reduced to a few frayed, smoking threads. And suddenly Alison was standing between Treasure and the linebacker chick.

"You gonna cry now?" Alison said to Treasure's tormentor, who now found herself standing on the edge of the freeway in boxer shorts and a camouflage-colored training bra, sniveling in fear and embarrassment while passing motorists honked and jeered.

The linebacker chick shook her head.

Gesturing to Treasure, Alison said, "You so much as look at her the wrong way and you *will* . . . You got me?"

The linebacker chick nodded and scurried off, still attempting to cover her exposed areas.

Alison gestured for Treasure to walk with her to the Mercedes that was parked nearby.

* ★ ★

David, Kellyn, and Designated Dean pretended to be interested in watching Dorinda perform card tricks on the hood of the car. In the backseat, Treasure sat mutely as Alison pulled off her white sunglasses and red hat.

"Remember me?" she said.

Treasure remained silent.

"No reason why you should," continued Alison. "You were horrible to me. But you've probably been horrible to a million other people and never given it a second thought."

Treasure gave Alison a defiant glare but still said nothing.

"Here's the difference. None of those million people are responsible for what's been happening to you. I am."

Treasure let out a little gasp. She started to climb out of the car. Alison put a hand on her arm. Treasure felt the heat and gasped again.

"I didn't *do* anything," Alison explained. "But I knew that someone was ruining your career and messing with your life, and I didn't stop it. I should have. You don't deserve this. No one does. Well, maybe that chick in the camouflage bra."

Treasure remained quiet. Alison shrugged. There was nothing more she could say.

"Okay. I'm done. I hope things go better for you in the future. I think they will."

Treasure got out of the Mercedes and walked back to the work crew. Feeling dissatisfied, Alison went to join her friends. Then Treasure Spinney turned around.

"Sundae Mundy!" she called out.

Alison looked over at her.

"That's what I'd call my ice-cream flavor. If Ben & Jerry ever called? When you interviewed me for *Jen*? When I was horrible. Caramel and pecan. It's spelled S-U-N-D-A-E. After the character I played on the show." Treasure rolled her eyes. "It makes sense if you see it written down."

"Sounds yummy." Alison smiled.

As Treasure rejoined the work crew, David, Kellyn, Dorinda, and Designated Dean broke into slow handclaps and fake sobbing.

"Once again, Saint Alison shows us lesser mortals how to rise above our petty jealousies," said Kellyn in a pious voice. But the expression on her face wasn't one of a bitter underminer.

They may have been mocking her, but they understood her. She was trying to accept everyone for who they were, flaws and all.

The clapping was suddenly drowned out by the roar of police sirens. One cop car roared down the freeway. Then two. Then three. More followed. The group exchanged glances. Something was *up*.

Designated Dean raced to his police scanner. The reception wasn't ideal. The voices coming over the scanner were crackly. But the situation was real. The deposed editor of the Beverly Hills High school paper had suffered a meltdown and taken the principal hostage.

"Oh My God," gasped Alison. "Lark Rise has gone bananas."

"You've been the most forgiving person alive for these past few weeks," said Kellyn to Alison as the Hottiemobile whizzed past the LAPD cars headed for BHHS. "You forgave T for abandoning you. You forgave Pixie for electrocuting you. You even forgave Treasure Spinney. So what are you gonna do when you get your hands on Lark Rise?"

Alison thought for a second. Then she grinned. "I'm gonna take her to my second-favorite restaurant chain." A second went by, and then she yelled out, "*Sizzler!*"

David burst out laughing. Then he brandished his phone and played the Hottie theme. Kellyn and Dorinda screeched along in shrill, faux-soulful voices. Designated Dean started beat-boxing in time to the rhythm.

Alison sat in the front passenger seat, listening to her friends mock her theme. She knew she would never stop missing T. But she was not alone. She had people who shared her secrets and her adventures. People who would race into danger with her without a thought for their own safety.

People who needed her and who she could confide in. She turned around and looked at them. At David. At Kellyn and Dorinda and even Double D. They were an amazing, instinctual, fearless, fantastic crime-fighting unit, and she'd never been so proud to call them her friends.

This time, nothing *can break us apart*, she thought.